FAR
BELOW
and other horrors

FAR
BELOW
and other horrors

edited *by* Robert E. Weinberg

 COLLECTOR'S EDITIONS

CONTENTS

INTRODUCTION

With the huge upsurge of interest in the supernatural and the occult in the last few years, there has been a corresponding increase in the number of collections of weird and fantastic literature. These anthologies fall into three basic categories.

The first, and probably most common, is the one-author collection. This type of book is satisfying in the sense that the collector or fan of the particular author can find a goodly number of stories by his favorite all in one place. However, there are several basic faults with this kind of book. Unless the author is an exceptional one, the book is a mixture of good, fair, and poor stories. Also, in an effort to make the most of the author's popularity, it is rare that all of his best stories are placed in one book. Lastly, in the case of the more popular weird fiction authors, their stories have appeared in so many other collections and anthologies that all but the most minor works are familiar to the reader.

The second type of grouping is the "classic" ghost story anthology. This book, often edited by a well-known personage, is an assemblage of famous horror stories such as "The Upper Berth" or "The Beckoning Fair One." Sometimes a slight nod is made to the modern with the inclusion of an H. P. Lovecraft story. The obvious fault with this sort of book is the familiarity of the stories as well as their easy accessibility in other sources. Also, stories are often picked not because of quality but because of the famous name of the author.

The third kind of horror collection suffers from this last-mentioned fault. Here we have a group of modern stories, those appearing in the last fifty years, many or all from the weird fantasy magazines of that period. The names of the contributors are familiar ones: Robert E. Howard, H. P. Lovecraft, Clark Ashton Smith, and others of the *Weird Tales* circle. The anthology suffers from either one of two faults. All of these authors are well known and their best stories have been reprinted many times. If the anthologist wants quality material, he is forced to reprint stories familiar to all but the novice collector. If, instead, he tries to present a group of stories by these well-known authors that are not familiar to the fantasy reader, he is forced to choose from stories that have not been reprinted for obvious reasons—either they are early stories written before the author learned his craft (oftentimes reprinted from fanzines or other amateur publications) or tales shunned by other anthologists because of their poor quality. In either case, the buyer is the loser.

In this book we have tried to assemble a modern anthology of weird fiction which avoids the pitfalls previously described. Instead of picking stories by the name of the author, we have chosen them by the quality of the piece. If the author is a famous one, so much the better. However, if the author is unknown and the tale a good one, the story remained. At the same time, we have tried to pick a group of stories that have not been over-anthologized.

Each story in this book has been picked for three basic reasons. The first factor in choosing a story is that it is a horror story. This book contains no tales of whimsy or humor. This is a collection of weird tales. At the same time, we have tried to avoid tales of gore and grue. Our contents range from the Lovecraftian horror of "Far Below" to the fantastic exploits in "The Chapel of Mystic Horror."

Our second consideration was rarity. All of these stories have appeared in professional print but all are relatively unknown to the average fantasy fan.

In the last few years, several people have written that there is little left in *Weird Tales* worth reprinting. These same people claim that the best stories have all appeared in anthologies and that only a few stories of note remain. Nothing could be further from the truth. Perhaps this situation is true in the case of well-known authors such as H. P. Lovecraft, but *Weird Tales* still harbors many a forgotten classic of horror or fantasy.

Another assumption made by these "experts" is that weird fiction fans own every anthology ever published in the field. Working on this premise, many fine stories have languished in rare old books, ignored because they have been reprinted once and the editor is looking to assemble a collection of "never before anthologized" stories. Several of the stories in this volume have appeared in other books but it is doubtful that any will be familiar to all but the most dedicated collector. Most of them have never appeared in any previous anthology.

Lastly, the stories in this book are meant to entertain. We make no claims that each and every story is a classic of great literature. Instead, we have striven to pick a collection of tales that will provide several hours of enjoyable reading. If that goal is achieved, our purpose will be fulfilled.

—Robert Weinberg

FAR BELOW

and other horrors

*Robert Barbour Johnson authored six stories for WEIRD TALES.
All of them are quite good but "Far Below" is his masterpiece.
In 1953, Dorothy McIlwraith, the editor of WEIRD TALES,
picked it as the best story ever to appear in the magazine. "Far
Below" has been reprinted only once before, and that was in an
anthology out of print for more than twenty years. The story has
lost not a bit of its terrifying impact since its original appearance
in 1939. The reader thus should be warned—this is not a story
to read while riding the subway!*

FAR BELOW

Robert Barbour Johnson

With a roar and a howl the thing was upon us, out of total darkness.
Involuntarily I drew back as its headlights passed and every object in
the little room rattled from the reverberations. Then the power-car was
by, and there was only the "klackety-klack, klackety-klack" of wheels
and lighted windows flickering past like bits of film on a badly-connected
projection machine. I caught glimpses of occupants briefly; bleak-eyed
men sitting miserably on hard benches; a pair of lovers oblivious to the
hour's lateness and all else; an old bearded Jew in a black cap, sound
asleep; two Harlem Negroes grinning; conductors here and there, too,
their uniforms black splotches against the blaze of car-lights. Then red
tail-lamps shot by and the roar died to an earthquake rumble far down
the track.

"The Three-One Express," my friend said quietly, from the Battery.
On time to the minute, too. It's the last, you know—until nearly dawn."

He spoke briefly into a telephone, saying words I could not catch,
for the racket of the train was still in my ears. I occupied the interval
by staring about me. There was so much to be seen in the little room,
such a strange diversity of apparatus—switches and coils and curious
mechanisms, charts and graphs and piles of documents; and, dominating
all, that great black board on which a luminous worm seemed to crawl,
inching along past the dotted lines labeled "49th Street," "52nd Street,"
"58th Street," "60th . . ."

"A new wrinkle, that!" my friend said. He had put down his phone
and was watching the board with me. "Lord! I don't dare think what
it cost to install! It's not just a chart, you know. It actually records!
Invisible lights—the sort of things that open speakeasy doors and rich
men's garages. Pairs of them spaced approximately every twenty-five
yards along five miles of subway tunnel! Figure that out on paper, and
the total you'll get will seem hardly believable. And yet the city passed

11

the appropriation for them without a murmur. It was one of the last things Mayor Walker put up before his resignation. 'Gentlemen,' he said to the Finance Board, 'it doesn't matter what you think about *me*! But this measure *must* go through!' And it did. There wasn't a murmur of protest, though the city was almost broke at the time . . . What's the matter, man? You're looking queer.''

"I'm *feeling* queer!'' I said. "Do you mean to say the thing goes that far back? To Walker's time?''

He laughed. It was a strange laugh, that died eerily amid the dying echoes of the train far down the tunnel.

"Good Lord!'' he gasped. "To his time—man, Walker hadn't served his first term as mayor when this thing started! It goes back to World War days—and even before that. The wreck of the train, I recall, passed as a German spy plot to keep us from going in with the Allies. The newspapers howled bloody murder about alleged 'confessions' and evidence they claimed they had. We let 'em howl, of course. Why not? America was as good as in the war anyhow, by then. And if we'd told the people of New York City what really wrecked that subway train—well, the horrors of Chateau-Thierry and Verdun and all the rest of them put together wouldn't have equaled the shambles that rioting mobs would have made of this place! People just couldn't stand the thought of it, you know. They'd go mad if they knew what was down here—far below.''

The silence was worse than the roar had been, I thought—the strange echoing, somehow pregnant silence of empty vastness. Only the "drip, drip'' of water from some subterranean leak broke it—that and the faint crackling noise the indicator made as its phosphorescent crawling hinted at "68th Street,'' "72nd,'' "78th . . .''

"Yes,'' my friend said slowly. "They'd go mad if they knew. And sometimes I wonder why we don't go mad down here—we who *do* know, and have to face the horror down here night after night and year after year—I think it's only because we don't really face it that we get by, you know, because we never quite define the thing in our own minds, objectively. We just sort of let things hang in the air, you might say. We don't speak of what we're guarding against, by name. We just call it 'Them,' or 'one of Them,' you know—take Them for granted just as we took the enemy overseas, as something that's just down here and has to be fought. I think if we ever really did let our minds get to brooding on what they are, it'd be all over for us! Human flesh and blood coldn't stand it, you know—couldn't stand it!''

He brooded, staring out into the tunnel's darkness. The indicator crackled faintly on the wall. "92nd Street,'' "98th,'' "101st . . .''

"Beyond 120th Street things are pretty safe," I heard my friend's voice as I watched. "When the train reaches that point you'll see a green light flash 'all clear,' though that doesn't mean absolute safety, you understand. It's just what we've established as the farthest reach of Their activities. They may extend them at any time, although so far They haven't done so. There seems to be something circumscribed about their minds, you know. They're creatures of habit. That must be what it is that's kept Them in this one little stretch of tunnel, with all the vast interlocking network of New York's subway system to rove in if they chose. I can't think of any other explanation, unless you want to get into the supernatural and say it's because they're 'bound' to this particular locality, by some sort of mystic laws; perhaps because it's lower than the other tunnels—chiseled far down into the basic bedrock of Manhattan, and so near to the East River you can almost hear the water lapping on quiet nights. Or maybe it's just the awful dankness of the tunnel here, the fungoid moisture and miasmic darkness that suits Them. At all events they don't come up anywhere else except along this stretch. And we've got the lights, and the patrol cars, and three way-stations like this one, with ten men on constant duty from dark till dawn—oh yes, my boy! It's quite a little army I command down here in the night watches—an army of the Unburied Dead, you might say; or an army of the Eternally Damned.

"I've actually had one of my men go mad, you know! Two others had to be placed in sanitariums for a while, but they got over it and are serving here still. But this fellow—well, we had to machine-gun him down like a dog finally, or he'd have got one of us! That was before we got the 'dark lights' placed, you see, and he was able to hide out in the tunnel for days without our being able to find him. We'd hear him howl sometimes as we patrolled, and see his eyes shining just as Their eyes do in the darkness; so we knew that he was quite 'gone.' So when we finally ran him down we killed him—just like that. No bones made about it. 'Put-put-put!' and that was the end. We buried him down in the tunnel, too, and now the trains run over him as he lies. Oh, there was nothing irregular about the business! We filled out full Departmental reports, and got the consent of his relatives, and so on; only we just couldn't take the poor fellow above-ground and run risks of people seeing him before interment. You see, there were certain . . . alterations. I don't want to dwell on it, but his face—well, the change was just beginning, of course, but it was quite unmistakable; quite dehumanizing, you know. There would have been some excitement up there, I'm afraid, just at sight of that face! And there were other details—things I only found out when I dissected his body. But I think

I'd rather not go into them either, old boy, if you don't mind . . .

"The whole point is, we have to be rather careful down here, all of us in the 'Special Detail.' That's why we have such unusual working conditions. We wear police uniforms, of course, but we aren't subject to ordinary police discipline. Lord! What would an above-ground 'cop' make of having every other night off and every day all to himself, and with a salary that—well, a corporal down here gets as much as does an Inspector up there!

"But, at that, I think we earn our pay . . .

"I know *I* do. Of course I can't tell you what my salary is—they made me promise never to disclose it when they hired me from the Natural History Museum back in—well, I don't like to think about how long ago that was! I was Professor Gordon Craig in those days, you know, instead of Inspector Craig of N.Y.P.D. And I'd just returned from Carl Akeley's first African expedition after gorillas. That was why they brought the Thing to me for examination, you see, after that first big wreck in the subway that'd only been opened less than a year. They'd found it pinned down in the wreckage, screaming in agony from their lights on its dead-white eyeballs. Indeed, it seemed to have died from the lights as much as from anything else. Organically it was sound enough, save for a broken bone or two.

Well, they brought it to me, because I was supposed to be the museum's leading authority 'on apes. And I examined it—believe me, I examined it, old boy! I went for six days and nights without sleep or even rest, analyzing that dead corpse down to its last rag and bone and hank of hair!

"No scientist on this earth ever had a chance like that before, and I was making the best of it. I found out all there was to be found before I collapsed over my laboratory table and had to be taken to the hospital.

"Of course long before that I had told them the thing wasn't an ape. There was vaguely anthropoid structure, all right; and the blood corpuscles were almost human—quite shockingly so. But the head and the spade-like appendages and the muscular development were quite unlike any beast or man on this earth. Indeed, the thing had never been on this earth! There was no doubt of that! It would have died above ground in half a minute, just like an angleworm in the sun.

"And I'm afraid my report to the authorities didn't help them much. After all, even a fellow scientist would have found it a bit difficult to reconcile my classification of 'some sort of giant, carrion-feeding, subterranean mole' with my ravings about 'canine and simian developments of members' and my absurd insistence on 'startlingly humanoid cranial development, and brain convolutions indicating a degree of intelligence that—'

"Well, there's no use going into all that now! I firmly expected them to order me up before a Sanity Commission when I reported my findings. Instead, they offered me a position as head of the 'Special Subway Detail,' at a salary that was, to say the least, fantastic. It was more a month than I'd been getting a year from the museum.

"Because, you see, they'd deduced much of the stuff for themselves without needing me to tell them! They had facts they'd deliberately withheld from me, not wanting to influence my report. They knew that that train had been deliberately derailed—the mutilated track proved that beyond all doubt. No less than three ties had been taken up and laid some distance away down the tunnel. And the condition of the earth about the wrecked cars showed conclusively that extensive mining and sapping had taken place there—it was like a gigantic mole-hill, only worse. And while I'd been analyzing stomach fluids and body tissue to try to find out what my subject fed upon, they'd been burying, secretly and with most elaborate precautions, the half-dessicated corpses of half a dozen men and women and children who—well, they hadn't died in the wreck, old boy! They hadn't died in the wreck, any more than had that screaming thing that hid its eyes from the lights when they found it pinned in the wreckage where it had been caught while trying to drag a dead victim out—God! What a hideous shambles that place must have been before the wrecking-crews got there.

"Mercifully, of course, there was total darkness. The poor devils who were merely injured never knew what charnel horrors were going on in the Stygian depths about them—nor cared, no doubt, in their agony! A few of them gibbered afterward about green eyes, and claws that raked their faces—but of course all that was set down to delirium! Even one man who had his arm chewed half off never knew—surgeons amputated the rest immediately and told him when he regained consciousness that he'd lost it in the wreck. He's still walking the streets today, blissfully ignorant of what almost happened to him that night.

"Oh, you'd be surprised, old boy, how you can hush a thing up if you've got a whole city administration behind you! And believe me, we *did* hush matters up. No newspaper reporter was ever allowed to see the wreck—freedom of the press or no freedom of the press! The Government wanted to appoint a commission to investigate—we squelched it! And by the time the crews had cleaned out the smashed train and removed the last victim, the Special Subway Detail had gone into action. And it's been on steady duty ever since—for the last twenty-odd years!

"We had a terrible time at first, of course. All these modern improvements weren't available then. All we had were lanterns and guns and hand-cars—with which to patrol nearly five miles of tunnel. It was Mrs. Partington sweeping back the sea all over again—only worse. A handful of puny mortals against Hell itself, in the eternal darkness of these long gloomy tunnels far below the city.

"There were no more wrecks after we took over, though; I'll say that much. Oh, an accident or two. How could we prevent them? We did everything we could think of! How we worked in those early years! Once we sank a shaft fifty feet deep in the earth, where we'd seen queer disturbances beside the train-tracks and heard queerer sounds. And once we blocked up both ends of the tunnel for a mile stretch and filled it with poison gas. And once we dynamited—but why go on? It was all useless, utterly useless. We just couldn't get to grips with anything tangible. Oh, we'd hear sounds sometimes on our long dismal patrols in the darkness; our little lanterns mere pin-pricks of light in these vast old concrete vaults. We'd catch glimpses of glinting eyes far off, find fresh earth piled up where only a moment before there'd been hard-packed cinders and gravel. Once in a while we'd fire our guns at something whitish and half seen, but there'd be only a tittering laugh in answer—a laugh as mirthless and savage as that of a hyena, dying away in the earth . . .

"A thousand times I was tempted to chuck the whole thing, to get back above ground to sunshine and sanity and forget the charnel horrors of this mad Nyarlathotep-world far underneath. And then I'd get to thinking of all those helpless men and women and children riding the trains unsuspecting through the haunted dark, with Evil out of the primeval dawn burrowing beneath them for their destruction, and—well, I just couldn't go, that's all. I stayed and did my duty, as the rest did, year after year. It's been a strange career for a man of science, and certainly one I never dreamed I'd be following during all the years I prepared myself for museum work. And yet I flatter myself that it's been rather a socially useful career at that; perhaps more so than stuffing animals for dusty museum cases, or writing monstrous textbooks that no one ever bothers to read. For I've a science of my own down here, you know: the science of keeping millions of dollars worth of subway tunnels swept clean of horror, and of safeguarding the lives of half the population of the world's largest city.

"And then, too, I've opportunities for research here which most of my colleagues above ground would give their right arms for, the opportunity to study an absolutely unknown form of life; a grotesquerie so monstrous that even after all these years of contact with it I sometimes doubt my own senses even now, although the horror is authentic enough, if you come right down to it. It's been attested in every country in the world, and by every people. Why, even the Bible has references to the 'ghouls that burrow in the earth', and even today in modern Persia they hunt down with dogs and guns, like beasts, strange tomb-dwelling creatures neither quite human nor quite beast; and in Syria and Palestine and parts of Russia . . .

"But as for this particular place—well, you'd be surprised how many records we've found, how many actual evidences of the Things we've uncovered from Manhattan Island's earliest history, even before the white men settled here. Ask the curator of the Aborigines Museum out on Riverside Drive about the burial customs of Island Indians a thousand years ago—customs perfectly inexplicable unless you take into consideration what they were guarding against. And ask him to show you that skull, half human and half canine, that came out of an Indian mound as far away as Albany, and those ceremonial robes of aboriginal shamans plainly traced with drawings of whitish spidery Things burrowing through conventionalized tunnels; and doing other things, too, that show the Indian artists must have known Them and Their habits. Oh yes, it's all down there in black and white, once we had the sense to read it!

"And even after white men came—what about the early writings of the old Dutch settlers, what about Jan Van der Rhees and Woulter Van Twiller? Even some of Washington Irving's writings have a nasty twist to them, if you once realize it! And there are some mighty queer passages in 'The History of the City of New York'—mention of guard patrols kept for no rational purpose in early streets at night, *particularly in the region of cemeteries*; of forays and excursions in the lightless dark, and flintlocks popping, and graves hastily dug and filed in before dawn woke the city to life . . .

"And then the modern writers—Lord! There's a whole library of them on the subject. One of them, a great student of the subject, had almost as much data on Them from his reading as I'd gleaned from my years of study down here. Oh, yes; I learned a lot from Lovecraft—and he got a lot from me, too! That's where the—well, what you might call the *authenticity* came from in some of his yarns that attracted the most attention! Oh, of course he had to soft-pedal the strongest parts of it—just as you're going to have to do if you ever mention this in your own writings! But even with the worst played down, there's still enough horror and nightmare in it to blast a man's soul, if he lets himself think on what goes on *down there,* below the blessed sanity of the earth's mercifully concealing crust. Far below . . .

"We've figured out—we who've been studying Them all this time, that They must have been pretty numerous once. No wonder the Indians sold this place so cheaply! You'd sell your home cheaply, too, if it were fairly overrun with monstrous noxious vermin that—but with civilization's coming they were decimated, killed off, pogromed against, blasted with fire and steel by men whose utter ruthlessness sprang from soul-shuddering detestation, who slew and kept silent about their slaying, lest their fellowmen think them mad—until finally the blasted remnant of the Things went far underground, burrowed down like worms to charnel depths that—well, we daren't conjecture just where, but we think that there's some fault in the basic bedrock of the Island, some monstrous cavern whose edge this lowest of all the subway tunnels taps, and which lets them through somehow into the tubes . . .

"Oh, it took us a long time to find all that out. At first we thought we had to patrol the whole subway system of the city! We had guards even out under the river, and over in Brooklyn and Queens. We were even afraid they'd get into upper levels of the tunnels, perhaps into the very deserted streets of Manhattan during the pre-dawn hours. We had half the police department down here in those days, even the mounted force. Yes, indeed; though God knows what even a trained police horse would do if it ever came face to face with one of those things! But horses were faster than the hand-cars we used then, and could cover more territory.

"But as time went on we got things pretty well localized. It's only in this one stretch of tunnel that the danger is, and only here in certain hours of the night. Don't ask me why they never come up in daylight; for it's always night down here, you know, hundreds of feet below the surface. Maybe it's the constant passage of the trains—they shuttle by at two-minute intervals all day long, you know, and until the Broadway theatres close at night. Only for about four hours of the night is there a lull when long miles of tunnel are lifeless and deserted and silent, when anything could come and go at will in them and not be seen.

"And so it's only during these hours that we really worry, you see. It's only now that we're vigilant and ready. Although of course it's no longer warfare, you understand. We hunt them now, they don't hunt us any more! We run them down howling with terror, kill them or capture them as we will—oh yes, I said capture! A half-dozen times we've had a sort of mad 'Bronx Zoo' of our own down here— or perhaps it would be more accurate to say a living 'Madame Tussaud's Chamber of Horrors.' I have cages in my laboratory, and there have been times when it seemed judicious for influential people above ground to—well, to realize just how important is the work we're doing down here! So when we have a really stubborn skeptic to our program we'd take him in there, hand him a flashlight and let him train it himself on what was prisoned there in total darkness—and then we'd stand by to catch him as he fainted! Oh, a lot of city officials and politicians have been down here. Why not? They couldn't possibly speak of the experience afterward—they'd just be locked up as lunatics if they did! And it made them much more liberal about funds. Our menagerie was a great success, only we just couldn't keep it going for very long at a time! We'd get so soul-sick at the very proximity of the creatures that we'd have to kill them finally. There was just no putting up with them for any length of time!

"Oh, it's not so much the appearance of the Things, or even what they eat—we got an unlimited supply of *that* from the city morgue; and to anyone who's spent half his life in dissecting-rooms, as I have, it might be a lot worse. But there's a sort of cosmic horror the Things exude that—well, it's quite beyond description. You just can't breathe the same air with them, live together in the same sane world! And in the end we'd have to gun them and throw them back underground to their friends and neighbors—who were waiting for them, apparently. At least we've opened the shallow graves a few days later and there'd be only a gnawed bone or two there. . . .

"And then, of course, we kept them alive in order to study their habits. I've filled two volumes with notes for my successors who'll carry on the fight when I'm gone—oh, yes, old boy! It'll always have to be carried on, I fear! There's no possibility of ever really wiping them out, you know. All we can do is hold our own. The fight will go on so long as this particular tunnel is occupied. And can't you just see the City Fathers consenting to abandon twenty million dollars' worth of subway tunnels for nothing? 'I'm sorry, gentlemen; but, you see, the place is infested with—' God! What a laughingstock anyone would be who even suggested that—above ground! Why, even on our own furloughs, when we walk sunlit streets among our fellow men, with God's own blue sky above and God's own clean air about us—even *we* wonder whether all this foulness isn't just a bad dream! It's hard, up there, to realize what can go on down in the crepuscular earth, the mad gnawing eternal darkness far below—Hello!''

The telephone was ringing.

Somehow I didn't listen as he spoke briefly into it, perhaps because I was listening to something else—to a faint crackling from that great blackboard on the wall, where one little light (no glowing worm this time, but only one minute spark) kept flicking oddly on and off and on again. "79th Street" it marked, over and over. "79th Street—79th—"

My friend hung up the phone at length, and stood up. "Queer," he said softly. "Very queer indeed! The first in months; and tonight, now, while we were talking. It makes one wonder, you know—about those supernatural telepathic powers that they're said to have . . ."

Something went past in the tunnel outside, something that moved so fast that I could scarcely make it out; just a little low platform on four wheels, with no visible engine to propel it. Yet it scudded along with the speed of a racing car. Uniformed men rode the bucking thing, crouching with glinting objects in their hands.

"Riot Car Number 1!" my friend said, grimly. "Our own version of the 'squad automobiles' above ground. Just one of the little electric hand-cars used in subway construction—but 'souped up' by our engineers until it'll do nearly eightly miles an hour. It could traverse the entire sector in less than five minutes, if it had to. But it doesn't, of course. Another one, also with machine-gunners aboard, left 105th Street at the same time. They'll meet somewhere along the tunnel's length—with the —er, disturbance in between. Let's listen to them!"

He crossed the room to the strange apparatus, threw switches and adjusted dials. There was a burring and crackling from what looked like an old-fashioned radio amplifier that stood on one of the cabinets.

"Microphones every hundred feet along the tunnel!" said my friend. "Another small fortune to install, of course; but another great step forward in our efficiency. A man listens all night long at a switchboard— and you'd be surprised to know what he hears sometimes! We have to change operators pretty often. Ah! there we are. Microphone Number 290—approximately a thousand feet below one of the busiest corners, even at this hour of the night, in all a great metropolis. And—listen! Hear that?"

"That" was a sound that brought me out of my chair, a strange high tittering, blasphemously off key, that merged into a growl and a moan . . .

"There we are!" my friend grated. "One of them, certainly—perhaps more than one. Hear that scratching, and the rustle of the gravel? All unsuspecting, of course, that they're broadcasting their presence; unaware that we modern human beings have got ourselves a few 'supernatural' powers of our own, nowadays; and unaware that, from both directions, death is sweeping down upon them on truckling wheels. But a little moment more and—ah! hear that shriek? That howling? That means they've sighted one of the cars! They're fleeing madly along the tunnel now—the voices get fainter. And now—yes! Now they double back. The other car! They're trapped, caught between them. No time to dig, to burrow down into their saving Mother Earth like the vermin they are.

No, no, you devils! We've got you! Got you! Hear 'em yell, hear 'em shriek in agony! That's the lights, you know. Blazing searchlights trained on dark-accustomed bodies; burning, searing, withering them like actual blazing heat! And now 'Brrr-rat-tat-tat!' That's our machine-guns going into action—silenced guns, with Maxims on them so that the echoes won't carry to upper levels and make men ask questions—but throwing slugs of lead, for all that, into cringing white bodies and flattened white skulls . . . . Shriek! Shriek, you beasts from Hell! Shriek, you monsters from the charnel depths! Shriek on, and see what good it does you. You're dead! *Dead!* DEAD— Well, you blasted fool, what are you staring at?''

To save my life I couldn't have answered him. I couldn't look away from his blazing eyes, from his body crouched as if he would spring at me across the room, from his teeth bared in a bestial snarl . . .

For a long moment that tableau held. Then suddenly he dropped into a chair, flung his hands up over his face. I stood regarding him, my mind sickly ticking off details. God! Why had I not seen them before. That lengthening of jaw, that flattening of forehead and cranium— no human head could be shaped like that!

At last he spoke, not looking up. "I know!" he said softly. "I've felt the change coming on me for a long time now. It's coming over all of us, bit by bit, but on me the worst, for I've been here the longest. That's why I almost never go above ground any more, even on leave. The lights are dim down here. But I wouldn't dare let even you see my face in sunlight!

"Twenty-five years, you see—twenty-five long dragging years down here in Hell itself. It was bound to leave a mark, of course. I was prepared for that. But, oh, Great Powers above! If I'd for one instant dreamed what it was to be! Worse, oh, how much worse than any mark of the beast! . . .

"And it's spiritual, you know, as well as physical. I get . . . cravings, sometimes, down here in the night's loneliness; thought and charnel desires that would blast your very soul if I were to whisper them to you. And they'll get worse, I know, and worse until at last I run mad in the tunnel like that poor devil I told you about and my men shoot me down like a dog as they already have orders to do if—

"And yet the thing interests me, I'll admit; it interests me scientifically, even though it horrifies my very soul, even though it damns me for ever. For it shows how They may have come about—*must* have come about, in fact, in the world's dim dawn; perhaps never quite human, of course, perhaps never Neanderthal or even Piltdown; something even lower, closer linked to the primeval beast, but that when driven underground, into caves and then beneath them by Man's coming, retrograded century by uncounted century down to the worm-haunted darkness—just as we poor devils are retrograding down here from very contact with them—until at last none of us will ever be able again to walk above in the blessed sunlit air among our fellow men—''

With a roar and a howl the thing was upon us, out of total darkness. Instinctively I drew back as its headlights passed; every object in the little room rattled from the reverberation. Then the power-car was by, and there was only the "klackety-klack, klackety-klack" of wheels and lighted windows flicking by like bits of film on a badly-connected projection machine.

"The Four-Fifteen Express," he said heavily, "from the Bronx. Safe and sound, you'll notice, its occupants all unsuspecting of how they were safeguarded; of how they'll always be safeguarded . . . but at what a cost! At what an awful cost!

"The Four-Fifteen Express. That means it's dawn, you know, in the city overhead. Rays of the rising sun are gilding the white skyscrapers of Manhattan; a whole great city begins to wake to morning life.

"But there's no dawn for us down here, of course. There'll never be a dawn for poor lost souls down here in the eternal dark, far, far below . . . ''

Julius Long was a Washington, D. C. fan who wrote many letters to WEIRD TALES as well as selling nine stories to the magazine. "The Execution of Lucarno" is the best of that group. The idea used, a unique one, was also expressed in H. P. Lovecraft's COMMON-PLACE BOOK, though it is doubtful that there is any connection between the two.

THE EXECUTION OF LUCARNO
Julius Long

He was a very ordinary looking young man of less than thirty. He might have been an office supply salesman or perhaps a bright young lobbyist come to bother the Governor with some sly request. He did not tell me his name but simply handed me his card.

I read: "Paul Barrett, M.D. Drexel Building."

"What can I do for you, Doctor Barrett?" I asked, tossing the card onto my table. It landed beside Dan Moultrie's feet cocked there.

"I wish to see Governor Mitchell."

"Have you an appointment?"

Being Governor Mitchell's secretary, I knew he hadn't.

"No."

"In that case, I'm afraid it's impossible for you to see him today. What did you want to see him about?"

"I want to see him about Hugo Lucarno."

I heard the creak of a chair and saw that Dan Moultrie was straightening up and eyeing the caller with interest. Moultrie was Lucarno's attorney and the best criminal lawyer in the state. He had a thin fox-like face and quick little eyes. He once told me that he'd always wanted to be a corporation lawyer but he didn't have any chance with a face like his. He'd been haunting the Governor's office for days trying to get a reprieve for Lucarno. Lucarno was the first client he'd ever had to be sentenced to the chair, and he was moving heaven and earth to keep his record clean.

"Why do you want to see the Governor about Lucarno?" I asked. "I hope you aren't one of those people who had a dream that convinced them he was innocent. Or maybe you want to pull the switch that electrocutes him tonight?"

"Yeah," said Moultrie, adjusting his tie. "What have you got to say about Lucarno? I'm his lawyer. If you've got anything I want to know what it is."

Doctor Barrett eyed us both coldly.

"I am not concerned with the guilt or innocence of Lucarno. I am

23

concerned only with a scientific experiment. If Governor Mitchell will permit me to make that experiment with Lucarno, I believe I can demonstrate the most startling discovery in the history of the science of psychology.''

I exchanged glances with Moultrie, who didn't bat an eye.

"What have you got?" he asked. "Some kind of a new lie detector?"

Doctor Barrett eyed him scornfully.

"No. As for the nature of my experiment, I can discuss that only with Governor Mitchell."

"I'm afraid you can't," I said. "The Governor happens to be a very busy man. I can't let you see him until I know whether he'd want to listen to what you've got to say."

Doctor Barrett looked at me with tilted brows and made a grimace with one side of his face.

"Very well. But I must speak with you privately."

"Listen," said Moultrie, "if you've got anything to say that concerns Lucarno, I'm in on it, see?"

"You can speak freely before Mr. Moultrie," I said quickly. "I'm sure that in any event Governor Mitchell wouldn't want to act without first advising Lucarno's attorney."

Doctor Barrett eyed Moultrie doubtfully, made another one-sided face an began to unfold his strange request.

"For a period of years," he said, "I have made a study of the psychology of fear. Of all the emotions, it is the most powerful. Its power, I believe, has never been more than superficially explored. In my study of it, I have been principally concerned with the fear of falling, which is beyond question the most primitive of all the fears to which the human race is susceptible. This, of course, is because our ancestors were arboreal, and the fear of falling from the limbs of the trees in which they dwelt was the most deeply rooted fear in their minds. It is significant that human infants react to only two fear stimuli, loud noises and the loss of support. Both stimuli induce a fear of falling, the former because the loud noise is associated with the cracking of breaking limbs."

I shot a quick glance at Moultrie. He was all ears. I decided that if he could give the doctor his attention, so could I.

"Perhaps," Doctor Barrett continued, eyeing us appraisingly, "you wonder why I have preoccupied myself with this fear of falling. My motive dates back to my first year of medical practice, four years ago. It was then that a strange accident occurred. An employee in the building in which I had my office fell down a freight elevator shaft when the safety device failed and allowed a door to open on the twentieth floor. The elevator car was stopped at the eighteenth floor, and its top was on a level with the nineteenth floor. The workman, then, fell only a single floor. Do you understand?''

I nodded. I might have said that I failed to understand how a workman falling through an elevator shaft could possibly concern Hugo Lucarno.

"The workman was killed," Doctor Barrett went on. "There was nothing intrinsically strange about that. Many men are killed by falls of less distance. The strange thing was that the workman was as badly crushed and mangled as if he had fallen the whole depth of the elevator shaft.

"The skull was crushed, the back was broken in several places, and there were compound fractures of both arms and legs. The muscles were horribly torn and lacerated, and the body was unrecognizable. I was the first physician called, and I refused to believe that he had fallen but a single story. The testimony of the several witnesses, however, convinced me that I was confronted with a distinct and thought-provoking phenomenon.

"The coroner dismissed the case as an ordinary accidental death. I think he knew there was nothing ordinary about it, but he didn't want to bother. I couldn't get the incident out of my mind. I pondered over it for days. Why, I asked myself time and again, was the body of that workman so horribly crushed?

"The phenomenon could not be explained by the simple reasoning that the effect of a fall depends largely on the angle or place of impact of the body. It is commonplace, of course, that men may fall five or six stories and live to tell about it. It is also a common occurence for people to slip on wet pavement and kill themselves. It depends on whether a vital spot takes the jolt. But to believe that a man who fell a single story down an elevator shaft could have been so horribly crushed and mutilated simply because of the manner in which he fell seemed out of the question. I decided that there must be some explanation to that phenomenon.

"It occurred to me that when the workman fell down that pitch-dark elevator shaft he must have thought he was falling clear to the bottom. I wondered if the state of his mind could have had any causal relation to the effects of his fall. Could it be possible that he had suffered the effects of a twenty-story fall simply because he *feared* he was falling twenty stories down that black hole of the elevator shaft?

"The more I considered such a possibility, the more I became fascinated by it. From idle conjecture it became an obsession. I began to seek a means of proving it.

"At length it occurred to me that interesting results might be obtained if I could create an optical illusion of great altitude. Would this optical illusion, I asked myself, cause a falling animal to suffer injuries entirely out of proportion to the distance it actually fell? Would its fear of the consequences produce the very consequences it feared? Would the psychological effect be so great that the body of the animal would lack its normal resistance to the impact? I resolved to make such an experiment.

"My initial difficulty lay in the creation of the optical illusion. Little is known of the chemistry of the optical nerves. I began a long series of experiments with compounds containing atropin, which affects only the parasympathetic nerves, and nicotine, which influences only the spinal sympathetic system. I experimented with myself, for I could not check the effects of drugs on animals except by external observation. My confidence in my hypothesis was so great that before taking these drugs I strapped myself to a pillar. I was convinced that if I succeeded in obtaining the illusion of great altitude I should become dizzy and fall. I expected no ordinary consequences from such a fall.

"At last I hit upon a formula which perfectly produced the illusion I sought. Strapped to a pillar, I found myself staring thousands of feet downward. The illusion was so perfect that despite my knowledge that I was safely strapped, I received such a fright that I was too weak to work for days. Upon my recovery I began to experiment with animals. The drug affected the guinea-pigs and cats and dogs and monkeys that I administered it to. I could assure myself of this from the terrified stare they fixed on the ground beneath them. Invariably they became dizzy and toppled over. And quite as invariably they shook themselves and walked away without injury.

"After months of failure, I had almost decided that my hypothesis was merely a wild flight of the imagination. Then it occurred to me that my failures might be ascribed to the kind of subjects I used in my experiments. I reflected that animals do not possess a consciousness at all comparable with that of human beings. It is a consciousness that is more instinctive than rational. Restricted by powerful instincts, it is less imaginative and less suggestible. My mistake lay in trying to explore the consciousness of human beings with the consciousness of animals. I might never hope to demonstrate the power of mind over matter with mind that was inferior to matter. In short, I could not conduct my experiments without human subjects.

"It seemed that I had reached a permanent impasse. If my experiment proved successful, the subject would die a horrible death. I had no doubt, of course, that there were plenty of skeptics quite willing to undergo the test. My hypothesis would seem so fantastic that no one would believe that he actually risked his life or even injury in acting as a subject of such an experiment. But I could not ask anyone to take such a risk, regardless of his willingness. I am not one of those cold-blooded scientists who will sacrifice human lives to prove an abstract theory. I am first a human being. Being human, I did not care, of course, to submit myself to the experiment. What then, was I to do?"

"I think I can answer that," said Moultrie. "You figured that Hugo Lucarno was going to die anyway, so it wouldn't make any difference what happened to him."

Doctor Barrett nodded.

"When I read about Lucarno in the paper this morning, I saw that I had the solution to my problem. Lucarno is a doomed man. He has nothing to lose. If the experiment is a failure, he will go to the chair as scheduled. If it proves a success, Lucarno will merely be paying his debt to society. Do you understand?"

I thought I did. I was face-to-face with a crack-brained scientist who wanted to waste Governor Mitchell's time with a fantastic request.

"There is only one thing the matter with your idea," said Moultrie sourly. "Lucarno isn't going to die in the chair tonight, or any other night. No client of mine has ever died in the chair, and none ever will. You can count on that."

"I'm afraid that stops you," I told Doctor Barrett, glad to be able to pass the responsibility. "Even if the Governor decided to let you try your experiment on Lucarno, he couldn't do such a thing without Lucarno's consent, and that means the consent of his lawyer."

"But," protested Doctor Barrett, "couldn't Governor Mitchell give me the authority anyway? I didn't imagine Lucarno would object. He seems to be a sort of devil-may-care fellow. The paper quoted him as saying that he was going to the chair unassisted, with a cigarette in his mouth and a smile on his lips. I believe that kind of fellow would submit voluntarily, as a sort of a lark. If the Governor would only ask him to do it, he wouldn't be depriving him of his rights."

I shook my head.

"The whole idea's out," I said. "The Governor would probably fire me if I even suggested it. As for his acting regardless of the wishes of Lucarno, he can't do it. Even a condemned murderer has certain rights. Among them is the right to die in the manner prescribed by law. You probably think that isn't much of a right, but I imagine that if you were in Lucarno's shoes, you'd change your mind."

"Then you won't even let me see the Governor?"

"No."

Doctor Barrett made that funny little one-sided face again, but didn't lose his temper. Aside from his crack-brained idea about falls, he seemed to be a pretty sensible fellow.

"In that case, I won't take any more of your time. Thank you for the time you've given me."

He turned on his heel and walked out. Dan Moultrie watched him go. Then he reached over and picked up the card Doctor Barrett had given me. He read it intently and tossed it aside.

"I wonder," he said musingly, "if that doc's got something."

"Just a crazy idea," I said.

"Maybe. And maybe not."

"I hope," I said, "you don't seriously believe that baloney you gave him about Lucarno's not going to the chair. That boy's going to fry tonight per schedule at eight o'clock, and you know it."

Moultrie breathed a long sigh.

"Yeah, it kinda looks like my shut-out record is ended. It looks like I'm licked. But maybe something will break for me before eight o'clock."

"You talk as if you were going to the chair instead of Lucarno."

"I'd about as soon," Moultrie said in a way that made me believe he meant it. "Maybe you don't know it, but I think I'm serving humanity by keeping murderers out of the chair. Yes, even a rat like Lucarno. Did you ever see a guy fry?"

I shook my head.

"Well, you ought to. Maybe you'd see why I think I'm not doing anything unethical by cheating the chair. Some day the Bar Association will stop denouncing me and unveil a monument to my memory."

"I'd like to see that," I said.

"You will, boy, you will."

Moultrie got out of his chair and moved toward the door.

"I'm not doing any good loafing around here," he said. "I'm going out and try to think. Maybe I'll get an idea."

I watched his frail figure disappear beyond the door. Then a buzzing sound made me move. Governor Mitchell was buzzing for me. He set me on an assignment that kept me busy all day. I didn't think anything more about Lucarno or Moultrie or Doctor Barrett until I bought a stock final at six o'clock. The Lucarno execution was big news. The news story hinted that Lucarno would get a reprieve, but I knew that was not true. The Governor had told me that morning that Lucarno was going to the chair regardless of anything Moultrie would try.

I finished reading the newspaper at the restaurant where I always dined. I was just getting ready to leave when Moultrie came back to my booth. It was seven o'clock then.

He sat down opposite me.

"I thought I'd find you here," he said.

"Well?"

"I'm going out to the state pen tonight," he said. "Lucarno's got to burn. I'm licked. I can't do anything to stop it. Mitchell's put the sign on me, and nothing I can do will change his mind. I've decided that I should be there when Lucarno takes his walk. I owe that much to him."

"Well?"

"I want you to go with me. I want you to see Lucarno when they pull the switch. Maybe you'll change your mind about a few things."

I stared at Moultrie, trying to figure him out. Why should he want to take me out to watch Lucarno die? Certainly he didn't care enough about my opinion to go to all this bother. He began to talk fast. Moultrie, when he wanted to be, was quite a talker. When he'd stopped talking, I'd agreed to go with him.

He drove out to the state prison in his low, fast convertible. It wasn't very far, for the state prison is on the edge of the downtown district. It was twenty minutes to eight when we arrived there. Moultrie had arranged for admittance, and we went right to the death house.

It was filled with newspaper men and officials. They sat on three benches facing the chair. I knew all of them, but felt so out of place in that gray room that it seemed to me I should be introduced all over again. It was fully five minutes before I could bring myself to look directly at the chair. I was surprised that I wasn't shocked by its appearance. It looked merely efficient.

At about ten minutes to eight, Moultrie left my side.

"I'm going to talk with Lucarno," he said. "Maybe I can say something to help."

A guard escorted him through a small door on the right. I sat there waiting, talking to the men around me but paying not the slightest attention to what anybody said. I felt hot inside and hoped I wouldn't get sick.

It was almost eight o'clock when Moultrie came back. He seemed nervous when he sat down beside me.

"It won't be long now," he said.

It wasn't.

The little door at the right opened, and a pair of guards stepped into the room. The warden followed, and then two more guards. Next was Lucarno.

He entered the death house precisely as he said he would, unassisted, with a cigarette in his mouth and a smile on his lips. It was a fresh cigarette, and had just been lighted. His collar was open at the throat, and he wore an unbuttoned vest. He looked as if he was on his way to answer a telephone that had interrupted a game of pool. Only a priest incongrously followed, along with another pair of guards.

"Hi, boys!" Lucarno said, his lips bobbing the cigarette around as he spoke.

Somebody coughed. Then there was absolute silence as Lucarno walked with a jaunty stride toward the chair. Out of the corner of my eye, I saw that Moultrie was watching him intently, expectantly.

The guards who had first entered the room now stood on either side of the chair. The warden stepped to its left. With a smirk, Lucarno moved to the chair. He turned around and faced us, whose hearts beat like tom-toms as we watched. He drew a long last puff from his cigarette and flicked it away. The guards moved toward him. Then Lucarno did a strange thing.

Abruptly he clapped his hands to his eyes. He held them there a moment, looked dazedly about him.

"I can't see!" he said, in a strange high-pitched voice. "I'm blind!"

The guards stopped in their tracks and looked questioningly at the warden. Was this some trick? The warden made no movement. He watched the condemned man, who was now staring downward *through* the floor, rather than at it. From a look of puzzled wonder, his expression became one of terror. His features assumed the distortion of a gargoyle, and his eyes receded into his skull as they seemingly stared into an abysmal depth. A figure of terror, he tottered as if on the brink of an abyss. And then, uttering a strangled cry, he fell forward.

His body struck the cement floor of the death house with a sound I shall never be able to forget. It was the sound of a body disintegrating into pulp. For Lucarno's skull became a flattened, spongy mass, and his body oozed through his ripped clothes.

How long the silence lasted, I do not know. Suddenly there broke out a pandemonium that roared in my ears. Newspaper men, yelling insanely, rushed to the narrow exit, collided there, struggled to press through. Presently, of the spectators, only Moultrie and I were left. I drew my eyes from the pulpy mass that had been Lucarno and looked at Moultrie. Chalk-white, he spoke to me in a low, almost inaudible voice.

"My God! Lucarno's as crushed as if he'd fallen a mile!"

"Did you see the way he stared?" I said. "He *thought* he was falling a mile. And the same thing happened to him that would have happened if he *had* fallen a mile! There's only one answer, Doctor Barrett."

Moultrie slowly nodded.

"I never dreamed," he mused more to himself than to me, "that such a thing could happen."

"What should we do?" I asked him. "Shouldn't we notify the police? This thing is murder!"

Moultrie's mind seemed to be working rapidly as he hesitated.

"Let's see Barrett first," he said. "We can call the police when we get there."

I stared quizzically into his little fox-like eyes.

"I think I see your point of view," I said. "You want to talk to Barrett before the police get there. You want to take his case. Is that it?"

"Maybe it is and maybe it isn't," he replied. "You might as well come along with me. There's nothing but chaos around this place, anyway, and I doubt if anyone would listen if we told what has happened. Come along. We'll have a talk with Barrett and see what he has to say."

For the second time that evening I let Moultrie persuade me against my better judgment. I accompanied him from the prison and got into his car. He drove rapidly, and in a very few minutes we were at the Drexel Building.

Before Moultrie left his car he drew a medium-sized automatic from the dash compartment and dropped it into his pocket.

"I may need this," he said.

I made no comment. But I failed to understand why Moultrie would need a gun if he intended to defend Barrett.

"Maybe Barrett won't be in his office," I said, as we entered the foyer of the building.

"He will be."

Moultrie seemed to know exactly what he was doing. He went directly to a phone booth and called police headquarters. I listened outside while he told them to send a squad at once to Barrett's office. While he made the call I tried to figure out just what his game was. I couldn't do it. But I knew he was playing some kind of lone hand.

In the elevator I asked him a question which had been in my mind since the thing had happened to Lucarno.

"How do you suppose Barrett managed to give Lucarno the drug? I can't see how such a thing could be possible."

"You'll soon know all about that," Moultrie said.

We left the elevator at the twentieth floor, where Barrett's office was located. There was a light shining through the frosted glass door of his reception room. Moultrie grasped the knob and pushed the door inward. We entered. Instantly an inner door opened, and Barrett stood there, eyeing us eagerly, expectantly.

"Well," he said excitedly to Moultrie, "what happened? Was the experiment successful?"

"Yes," said Moultrie. "The experiment was successful. Lucarno was mashed to a pulp because he thought he was falling a mile from the sky."

"I knew it!" Barrett exclaimed jubilantly. "I knew it! At last the power of fear has been demonstrated! It is the greatest discovery in the science of psychology. I wonder what these mechanistic psychologists will have to say about this!"

"I want to talk to you," Moultrie said, moving toward the inner door.

Barrett stepped aside. I followed. Moultrie closed the door behind him when he had entered Barrett's private office. I went directly to a water-cooler in one corner and drank two glasses of water. I felt better.

"Have a cigarette," said Moultrie, extending an opened case. "It will steady your nerves."

I took one and lighted it. When I had finished lighting it I saw that Doctor Barrett was staring quizzically at me. Then he turned and opened his mouth to question Moultrie. The words did not come, and as I followed the direction of his gaze, I saw why. Moultrie had the automatic in his hand and he was aiming it directly at Barrett. Even as I saw the gun, Moultrie squeezed the trigger twice.

Barrett looked a little bewildered, then settled down on the floor. He coughed once or twice and lay still.

I stood there watching, puffing madly on my cigarette. Then I fairly shrieked at Moultrie.

"Why in the name of God did you do that?"

Moultrie removed his eyes from the motionless body. He lifted them slowly to my own.

"I had to," he said. "You see, I have a strong instinct of self-preservation. If Barrett had lived long enough to be arrested, he would have told the police that it was I who gave Lucarno a drugged cigarette before he walked to the chair and made the experiment possible."

"You!"

"Yes. It was my last card. I had to play it in a desperate effort to get the execution stayed. I went to Barrett after I left your office this morning and told him I would give Lucarno the drug. I told him that if Lucarno was killed, I could get him acquitted. Of course, I would be an accomplice in case Lucarno was killed, but I never dreamed he would be. I thought the drug would just make him dizzy and fall over. I hoped he'd break an arm or injure himself some other way so badly that the execution would have to be stayed. You're probably familiar with the state law that a man cannot be executed unless he is sound physically—permanent disabilities not counting, of course. I intended to invoke this law if anything happened to Lucarno. I could get the execution stayed, and that would give me more time to have the sentence commuted. But it turned out that Barrett's theory about fear was right, and Lucarno was killed. You see what a spot that put me in.

"I knew Barrett wouldn't keep his mouth shut. He'd want everyone to know what a great scientist he is. So I had to kill him. I had to do it sooner than I planned, because he was about to say that I had given you one of the cigarettes he had prepared for Lucarno. You see, I have to get rid of you, too. When the police come I will tell them that Barrett gave you the cigarette and attacked me when I saw what happened to you. I had to shoot him in self-defense."

Moultrie's little eyes were fixed on the cigarette I held between my lips. In the excitement of Barrett's shooting, I had been puffing it madly. Now, as the truth came to me, I tore it from my mouth and flung it to the floor.

"It's too late," Moultrie said softly. "The drug is already in your system."

"You swine!" I shouted. I started for him, ignoring in my anger the gun in his hand.

Half-way toward him, I halted. Everything in the room faded abruptly into grayness. Then quite as quickly vision returned to me.

But what a vision! The floor of that office had become a wide, boundless plain, and its walls were beyond its horizon! I was suspended thousands of feet above it by some inexplicable means. The incredible part of it was that I actually believed this to be a fact! My terror was complete, overwhelming. It would not permit me to reflect for an instant that all was an optical illusion, that I stood safely on the floor of Doctor Barrett's office. The doctor, Moultrie, the events of the evening, all were blotted out of my consciousness. I was aware only of that horrible altitude at which I remained suspended in the air. My dizziness increased geometrically with my terror. I knew that I must fall. I had to fall. It was useless to try to retain my balance there in the sky. Vertigo was pulling me irresistibly downward. And when I fell . . .I recalled vaguely a shapeless form oozing from exploded garments upon a cement floor. That was the way I would be when I fell down there, thousands of feet below. I tottered now and tried in vain to right myself. I started that inevitable plunge forward.

But something clutched me above my knees, held me there in space. I righted myself, stood erect again. I heard a violent oath and then a blinding flash caused me involuntarily to close my eyes. I held them so tightly closed that they pained me almost unendurably as the support about my legs gave way. The horrible illusion of altitude left me, and I felt my feet firmly planted on the floor again. I must, I realized now, keep my eyes closed, or that illusion would return to me with vision.

Bony fingers were clawing at my face now, and I realized with horror that Moultrie was trying to pull my eyelids open! I struck out and landed a solid blow. I heard a body falling. I groped about blindly and presently felt a doorknob in my grasp. I opened a door, staggered from the room. Somewhere a siren was sounding. I kept on groping, striking the walls, but going blindly on.

I was in the corridor when the police officers found me. They held me while I dared to open my eyes. Normal vision had returned to me. I led them to Doctor Barrett's office.

Doctor Barrett lay on the floor of the room. He was not where I had last seen him, and I knew that it had been he who had gripped my legs and thus prevented my falling. A third bullet had ended his life. It was the firing of this bullet by Moultrie that had blinded me and caused my eyes to close.

It was the thing in the corner that drew the attention of the police. The mangled body of Moultrie gave mute testimony that the lawyer had given up his case as hopeless. His death was incomprehensible to the police officers, who failed to grasp the significance of the cigarette which was still clutched in his pulpy hand.

G. G. Pendarves was a pseudonym for Gladys Gordon Trenery, an English authoress who died in 1939. Her nineteen stories published in WEIRD TALES have all but been forgotten, even though all are quality works. Ms. Trenery usually wrote horror stories with a strong occult background, a subject with which she showed a great deal of familiarity. The following tale, however, is more in keeping with her homeland. It is an old-fashioned ghost story.

THING OF DARKNESS
G.G. Pendarves

I

A long curving sweep of tall gray houses. At their feet the old parade, its worn seawall banked up against wind driven tides. Troon House, grayer, gaunter than the rest, stood empty. A signboard creaked on rusted hinges, advertising it For Sale or To Let.

Lonely. Lovely. Deserted.

Seagate was proud of Troon House. Seagate was afraid of it. People came by the score to see it, always in broad daylight. They were careful to keep in groups, silent, timid, turning a sharp corner, entering each unexplored room with that sudden jolt that a clumsily manipulated elevator gives to one's heart.

They stared at beautiful restorations, at blackened beams, at vast wall-cupboards, and at brick fireplaces whose ancient clay showed every tint of umber, rose and purple-brown. They bunched together closely going up the last steep narrow stairs to the west attic. They looked at its deep recess, recently and fatally uncovered—looked and shuddered.

They went in close order downstairs again, escaped through low-roofed, retiled kitchens to a long untended garden behind the house and thence to a broad lane and main road at last. Shaken, nervously loquacious, they didn't speak of Troon until the old place was out of sight. Over tea and famous Seagate shrimps they exchanged impressions.

Going home after sunset, if they stayed so long, they glanced in passing along the road, at Troon's blank front windows, shivered, looked quickly away.

Troon—gray old house, left to hideous memories of the Thing of Darkness. Day by day, night by night, through the years, through the centuries Troon had stood. Old, forsaken, betrayed. Old Troon—shell of death—old Troon.

Low sullen clouds. A cold northwest wind. Fierce squalling gusts of rain. A high angry tide, gray-green flecked with bitter white, roaring up the estuary. Seagate was a mile of wet gray road and blank-faced houses. Wind and sea . . . wind and sea.

At the village-church of Keston, a fifteen minutes walk away on the hill behind, the broken body of Joe Dawlish with its staring tortured eyes and twisted face of fear was being buried. And in another grave, a sad small grave, the bones of Lizzy Werne were being laid to rest after three hundred years delay.

People thronged the small churchyard to its broad low moss-stained walls. From Seagate, from Keston, from all over the Wirral peninsula, and even from Liverpool and Chester they had come to witness this double funeral. Reporters, psychic investigators, university professors rubbed wet shoulders with fishermen, farmers, shop-keepers and local gentry.

At the end, the very end when the last words of the service were said and it only remained for the gaping graves to be filled in, the vicar stood with uplifted hands. His somber gaze looked out over the crowd to tossing trees and lowering sky. His lined face, wet with rain, was worn and anxious.

Suddenly his voice rang out again, a cry from the heart of this shepherd of a stricken flock . . . "Deliver us, O Lord, from all assaults of the devil! In thine infinite mercy, protect and succor us! Stretch forth thy hand against this Thing of Darkness and set us free from fear! In the name of Him who died for us—Amen."

There was a murmurous response like water breaking on a distant shore. Then, slowly, silently, pelted by spiteful icy rain, the crowd dispersed.

At the lich-gate Doctor Dick Thornton was pushed up against two people he wanted to avoid: Edith and Alec Kinloch. Alec's heavy sallow face showed distinct traces of emotion. He looked quite appealingly at Doctor Dick.

" 'Fraid I didn't take all this quite seriously before," he confessed. "I don't understand what it's all about, but—"

Edith put a restraining hand on his arm. He was having one of his emotional moments, she could see. Heaven knew what he might say! Probably he would double his already absurdly generous offer of five pounds to the widow. What a blessing she could count on herself never to lose her head! Queer sort of service it had been. These villagers adored emotional orgies. Well, poor things, they must have some pleasure in their dull stupid lives. Clever of the vicar to stage such a good show for them. He knew how to cater for a rural diocese.

To deflect her husband from possible weakness she turned to the young girl behind her.

"Lynneth, this is Doctor Thornton. He's a sort of uncle to all the fishermen of Seagate. Miss Lynneth Brey, Doctor Thornton. A connection of my husband's. She's going to spend a month or so with us—at Troon."

There, Edith thought, that'll let him know right off that they've not succeeded in scaring us. Her tactics were wasted. The doctor didn't even hear her. He was looking down into Lynneth's uplifted rosy face. Black eyes, soft, sooty, heart-catching. Eyes made for tears and laughter and —oh, yes! he knew at once—made for love. He looked deep, deeper into them; young, radiant, kindled with recent deep emotion. Eyes to light a man's path, to draw him on and up, above life's dusty sordid clamor. Eyes that promised and withheld.

Doctor Dick's feet were treading air, his heart thumped with the beat-beat-beat of hooves on a hollow road, his head felt full of fizzy champagne. But no one guessed it. He heard his voice, it didn't seem to surprise anyone, replying to the introduction. He waited with parted lips, eyes a clear tender blue, listening—listening for her voice.

"Oh!" She considered him. A smile drew her lips in an adorable sideways quirk. "You make me feel homesick, although I've only been here a day. You speak like a Highlander."

"I am one. From Gairloch."

She put out a small hand to be enveloped in his close grip, and laughed in quick delight.

"That's my place. My own darling funny village. My mother's birthplace. We've got a cottage there. D'you remember it—the one like a brown loaf at the head of Glen Ruach?"

They drifted from the churchgate, away down the twisting road. The crowd of people might have been blown wet leaves. The two Kinlochs, left behind, exchanged long glances.

"Let 'em go." Alec took his wife's arm. "Birds of a feather—eh? She and Pills can keep each other amused. Looks like a case to me. You won't be bothered with her long."

"Really, Alec! There's the garage—what on earth are you dragging me on for? I'm certainly not going to hang about for that silly girl. Going off with a man she's just met, like that! She behaves like a child. No idea of appearances."

"What odds? Nobody's going to notice a kid like that."

"Nonsense! She's connected with us. D'you want him for a permanent relation?"

"Why not? Get the girl off your hands while the going's good. She and Pills would run a dispensary or a nursing-home and be too busy to interfere with us. This yearly visit's beginning to pall."

She glanced shrewdly at him.

"Something in that. And even if he's queer, quite important people have taken him up. Come on, then. I'm perishing with cold. This sensed fuss! Seagate doesn't seem to have altered since Troon House was first built."

They clambered into their car and splashed down the lane to their bungalow by the marshes.

"Quite! Quite! However, there are always two sides to everything."

Mr. Alec Kinloch presented a large bulwark of flesh from behind which his schoolboy's mind issued bulletins to the outside world. He kept a store of such ready-made bulletins within, stereotyped responses calculated to give intimation of a subtle discerning intellect at work. He would employ such tactics indefinitely if conducting a conversation un-aided. If his wife was with him she manned the big guns while he posed as an impregnable fortress.

Doctor Dick regarded the large dull pretentious creature with patience born of his profession rather than his temperament. Doctor Dick was a Highlander. Alec Kinloch a Lowland Scot. This, in itself, was a deep fixed gulf between them, apart from gulfs of breeding and intellect, and today the doctor found his host peculiarly trying. He'd made a point of calling when he knew Lynneth would not be at Sandilands. He wanted to spare her the grim tale he had to tell. It had been an effort, however; to miss a chance of seeing her, and his mood grew steadily darker.

"What," he demanded, "would you consider the other side of this horror at Troon?"

Baffled at such direct attack, Alec poked at his pipe with an air of grave reserve. He and Edith always were careful to be non-committal in their attitude until they discovered the trend of popular feeling with reference to a new idea. This Troon ghost notion now! If Seagate took it seriously, and yesterday's funeral service seemed to indicate so, then they would follow suit. Alec had been swayed by the vicar yesterday. Now, however, he knew Edith's view was the really intelligent and logical one. The vicar had been simply playing up, doing what the villagers expected of him. Jolly good thing no one but his wife knew that he'd actually got the wind up yesterday. The "Thing of Darkness!" Uh! Nasty phrase that! He'd felt like chucking up everything—selling Troon to any fool who wanted the old place. Well, he could laugh at himself and his fears now.

But this young Pills! He seemed officious. Trying to interfere. Pulling all this stuff about haunts and devils at Troon. Warning him that the workmen restoring the old house were in danger and that he and Edith ought to give up all idea of living there. Damned young whippersnapper, sitting there at his ease and telling a man of the world what was what! He'd tell him where he got off all right!

The door opened to admit his wife. Alec crossed his legs, resumed his pipe, took up the fortress-pose as Doctor Dick rose to his feet. Edith Kinloch progressed with ceremony to a chair.

"How nice of you to call again—so soon, Doctor Thornton."

"Doctor Dick" corrected the visitor. "My father is still in practice here. We have to make a distinction."

"Oh! How awkward for you!"

Edith was slim and tall and neat. She was invariably bright and kind too. It was part of her chosen role to stoop kindly to her inferiors. The Lady Bountiful was her favorite part, to be gracious, to condescend. She'd been these things infuriatingly and increasingly ever since she cut free from her decent but quite uneducated family at the age of fourteen. Alec never knew to this day that her mother had a fish-and-chips shop in Edgware road, that her father was crippled and on the dole, that her younger sisters were working in a glue factory.

"My wife," Alec would tell you, believing it to be a fact, "lost both her parents—died in India when she was a child. Friends made themselves responsible for her education" (the Local Educational Council as represented by Edith's adaptable mind) "a branch of the Dorsetshire Frome-Stoddarts, you know. Good old family but improverished—improverished."

Edith smiled brightly on the two men sitting before the study fire.

"I'm sure you must be cold and hungry, Doctor—Dick, if you insist on the familiarity. I just went to tell cook she must drop everything and make some of her famous hot cakes for tea. Cook is so difficult, but really I find the best thing is to alter her routine every now and then. I do it on principle."

She proceeded to stage-manage a background for an afternoon-tea act. Doctor Dick was used as scene-shifter. Edith directed him with firm smiling competence. He pulled up tables and pushed away chairs. She conveyed atmospherically that he was young and insignificant enough to do these things rather than Alec.

"And now do let's go on with all that too adorable tale you were telling us about Troon just now. So like a story of Edgar Allan Poe's. Now don't say you finished that tale while I was out of the room! No? That's right!"

She beamed approval.

"Now. We're all settled. Tea—and put on another log, Alec, the basket's beside you there—a real Christmas fire to warm you up, Doctor

Dick. And eat up the scones; you must be needing something. No use calling at teatime and not taking advantage of the fact.''

Glittering gracious hostess. Her varnished toffee-brown eyes shone in the firelight. She addressed the doctor as if he were a schoolboy out for a treat. She was convinced he'd arranged purposely to call at their tea hour. So lean and hungry-looking! She plumed herself on the observation which thus misread Doctor Dick's rigidly disciplined muscular body.

"This is the only time I can call," the doctor was young enough to feel not amused at her patronage. "I pass this bungalow on my way up to Keston. Due at the hospital at five, you know."

Edith smiled her best worldly understanding smile. Let the young man get away with his excuses, poor dear. She didn't grudge him his tea. Pity Lynneth was out. It would have been easy then to sidetrack him from the mission he felt he had concerning Troon and its restoration. She must make things plain, perfectly plain, once and for all. She leaned forward. Her glistening eyes, her perfectly smooth face, her small ungenerous mouth registered smiling cordiality.

"Now do tell me all about it."

Doctor Dick's blue eyes grew black and gray as the November afternoon. He told her. Told her details of Joe Dawlish's death. Told her of daily increasing peril at Troon. Implored her to give up the whole thing, to leave the gray haunted old house to its evil.

"The men are in hourly danger—horrible danger. You are letting loose forces that· have been pent up in the place for centuries. The men should come off the job at once."

At his increasingly urgent manner, Alec and Edith Kinloch stiffened simultaneously. After all, dash it all, the house is mine, ran Alec's thoughts, and there's a limit to the interference one can stand! Edith's eyes answered his unspoken protest, agreeing with it.

Alec voiced his ideas. His tone was a subtle reproach.

"Was this Joe Dawlish working on the house when he died?"

"He was." The doctor's clipped reply roused all Alec's fathomless obstinacy.

"I suppose he was insured."

Alec's own instant perception of the vital core of this queer fuss about Dawlish gratified him enormously. He was moved, without waiting for his wife's lead, to make a gesture.

"Well, I might give the wife a little extra. Ten pounds would pay for the funeral—handsomely. These people love a ghoulish sort of feast, don't they? 'Buried him with ham'—what!"

"Ham? Er, yes . . . quite. Ham."

Doctor Dick looked his host up and down as if he saw some connection between him and the word he reiterated. He got to his feet.

He was out of the room, out of the little entrance-hall, out of the house—stalking like a longlegged bird down the garden and on to the road almost before Edith and Alec could reply to his swift farewell. He'd been so quick, so cumbered with hat, stick and a knobby untidy parcel, that he didn't even shake hands.

Alec threw himself down in his armchair by the fire, took up a brass toasting fork and began to warm up the remaining scones. Edith watched him absent-mindedly.

"Shut Pills up, didn't I?" he spoke with his mouth full of scone. "Nothing like getting down to brass tacks with these fellows. Driveling about spooks and Troon! Neat dodge for collecting for Dawlish's widow. Better do the thing handsomely, as we're strangers here. Living at the big house, we'll be obliged to play up a bit."

Edith continued her pursuit of abstract thought.

"Well?"

"Yes, dear."

She came out of her trance, sat forward inelegantly, a thin hand on either knee. Strong emotion did occasionally uncover the past.

"Alec, there's more in this than meets the eye. Mark my words, there's someone else after Troon. They want to turn us out, force us to sell. I dare say they've found how old and much more valuable the property is than they believed. Let 'em try!"

He wolfed the last scone, pulled out a large white linen handkerchief, polished his lips, arranged his mustache, hitched up his trousers at the knee and lighted a fresh pipe.

"Let 'em!" he echoed in profound sepulchral tones.

Six o'clock on a late November evening. Rain and a squalling wind from the east. A high tide slapping and hissing against the mile-long ancient seawall.

Jim Sanderson drove at his job in the cold drafty house with nervous hurry. A highly intelligent able workman was Jim, the best workman of the gang at Troon House.

Well over three hundred years old the house was. Of late it had fallen into bad disrepair. Its landlord lived in Ireland and had rented his fine old derelict to one careless tenant after another until roof and walls let in as much weather as they kept out.

The Liverpool agent happened to love the house. He had done his best, wrested small sums from its owner for patching here and patching there for forty odd years. But he and Troon could bluff no longer.

Would-be tenants kept on coming, for a genuine old Seagate house for sale was rare. Their verdict was unanimous. Damp! Rain drove in through deep cracks and faulty windows. Salt water used in the cement made ugly discolorations everywhere. Timbers were rotting. One roof had curvature of the spine. Toads and spiders had taken over ruined outbuildings and kitchens. Weeds, coarse grass, overgrown hedges and dumps of rubbish made a desert of the long garden at Troon's back.

At last, the agent had put up enormous startling bills in each of Troon's front windows. And, suddenly, he sold the house.

The two Kinlochs had seen it. They had money. They needed an old and mellow background. They got a first-class architect to vet the place, found a reasonable sum would make it weatherproof, beat the Irish landlord down a little—very little, for he was savage as a cornered rat. Followed a flurry of contracts, plans, and agreements, then parleyings with the local council, who mistrusted haste and people with money to spend on a damp derelict house in Seagate. And the Kinlochs were in a hurry: they wanted to settle in before Christmas.

At last Troon House legally changed hands. The Kinlochs rented a bungalow lurking a mile away by the marshes. Troon was delivered up to the builders and decorators.

And so we return to Jim Sanderson on this gloomy November evening.

He had an electric torch, for no light was yet installed in the house. By its beam he prodded furiously at a patch of decayed timber by the hearthstone. A specimen was demanded by the Mycology Section of the Forest Products Research Laboratory. Dry rot was suspected in this large front room on the ground floor. Sanderson had to send his specimen by that night's post. The other workmen were gone. He was working overtime—alone.

Clap! Clap! Clap!

Somewhere in the drafty darkness upstairs a door banged persistently. It got on his nerves. He was a sensitive man in spite of his big muscular frame. Temperament, imagination, nerves were part of his quick flexible intelligence. He hated this night job. He felt queer and jumpy.

Clap! Clap! Clap!

There! The damned door had shut itself at last. He heaved a sigh of relief. Then his scalp prickled. Was someone up there? Had they shut the door? Was that someone coming down the broken creaking staircase?

The whites of his eyes showed like those of a frightened horse as he glanced up at the rainblurred glass of a large bay-window on his right. Impulse seized him to dash himself at the panes, to escape to the friendly old parade just outside. Overwhelmingly he wanted to be out in the open—to exchange this dusty, musty shelter for rain and salt wind and flying scuds of foam.

He'd had enough. Things had got worse ever since Joe Dawlish had pulled down the cupboard in the big west attic a week ago. The wall and chimney-breast had crumbled and broken with its removal. A few stout blows, and the whole false facade had come down, revealing a deep recess reaching from rafters halfway to floor. On the broad stone shelf thus formed, a skeleton lay.

The bones of a child. Skull smashed in. A staple and chain padlocked round the bone of the left arm. The padlock was the strangest thing of all, of black smooth heavy stone with queer red markings chalked on it.

The vicar had been summoned in a hurry. He'd brought Doctor Dick with him. They were in a great taking about the affair, and carried off the poor little bones for burial.

From that hour things had gone wrong at Troon. Joe, who'd found the bones, was dead and buried inside a week—and what a week, too!

Sanderson's big brown hands fumbled as he tugged and strained at the flooring. He felt suddenly hot and weak. There was a flurry in his brain. He wrenched out the piece of wood he needed, stowed it roughly away in a torn capacious pocket of his old coat. Still on his knees, he gathered up his tools.

He rattled and banged things about, trying to shut out other sounds . . . sounds on the stairs . . .

The breath seemed to stop in his big body.

Creak. Creak. Creak.

It was someone cautiously stealing downstairs.

Crack!

He knew that sound. It was a broken step, third from the bottom. He tried to call out. It must be that damned oaf, Walter! The fool must have gone to sleep up there. Sanderson couldn't make his stiff dry tongue obey him. He couldn't hail whoever it was out there. He couldn't —he daren't.

His hunted eyes sought the window. Power to move, to jump for it, had left him. He knelt there, powerful shoulders hunched, hands on the floor for support, crouched like a big frightened animal. He fought to prevent himself looking over his shoulder at the door behind. He knew it was opening. He heard stealthy fingers on the old loose knob. He heard the harsh scrape of wood on wood as the sagging door was pushed back.

Ice-cold wind blew in, rustled bits of paper and shavings on the floor.

Sanderson's head jerked back to look. The door stood widely open. His eyes, filmed with terror, focused achingly on the gap between door and wall. Darkness moved there. A Thing Of Darkness. On the threshold it bulked in shapeless moving menace. Darkness made visible . . . blotting out everything . . . blotting out life itself.

The crash of a small wooden crate on which his heavy hand rested saved Sanderson from fainting. He leaped for the window. Glass cracked and fell in sharp tinkling showers. A thick cloth cap protected his lowered head. He was through. He fell on the strip of trampled grass outside, among a tangle of ladders and buckets. He vaulted the pointed iron railing and was in the road—running—running—breath coming in deep sobbing gusts—deathly face splashed with rain and blood.

Ahead shone the cheerful red and white lamp of the Three Mariners. He went straight for it as a fox for a familiar burrow.

Mr. and Mrs. Burden—old Tom and old Mary to most—who kept the Three Mariners were sitting in their vast red-tiled kitchen before a blazing fire. Black hand-made rugs were spread. Oil lamps of heavy brass hung from massive black oak rafters. At a round walnut table covered with a crimson cloth, Mrs. Burden was working placidly through a pile of stockings to be mended. Solomon, a great tawny Persian cat, dozed with its leonine head on her instep. Mr. Burden, smoking a long churchwarden, sat in a wide Windsor chair glossy with age and use, his stockinged feet on a gleaming wrought-brass stool.

Doctor Dick sprawled on a settle near by. Two or three fishermen, warming up before the tide turned and they put out for their night's catch, completed the little company of friends.

They all looked up at the loud bang of the outer door. Every face was turned toward the kitchen entrance when Jim Sanderson burst in.

"For God's sake—a drink!"

He collapsed into a big chair and sat with head down on his hands, shivering and gasping before the hot fire. Doctor Dick was at his side in a moment. Mrs. Burden ran for a drink. Mr. Burden dropped his favorite pipe and stared. The fishermen sat forward, hands on knees, consternation on their weathered red-brown faces. Solomon stood with arched back, great feathery tail waving nervously, before seeking shelter under a distant chair to await developments.

Sanderson told his experience in jerks between sips of the Three Mariners' best Jamaica rum. His audience blinked, muttered, stared. Doctor Dick, that brilliant modern young man, listened with flattering and tremendous concentration, seablue eyes and keen face losing every trace of their habitual friendly good-humor.

Mrs. Burden sat immobile. She had, as always, a flavor of the wild, of a remote and more instinctive age, of ancient beliefs and wisdom. She moved like a feather in a draft of wind—so light, so frail, so incalculable. She always seemed curiously unrelated to furniture and rooms and human dwelling-places in spite of making the Three Mariners the coziest inn in the whole county of Cheshire. She had the quality of some dear deep peatbrown river, nourishing the earth and nourished by it.

Her husband, rocklike as she was fluid and quick, turned to her now.

"What d'yer say to that, old woman? That there Troon house was always what you might say queer-like. I reckon it's had queer folk in it and all. But I never heard tell of anything out and out bad."

"No? Well, I did, then."

Doctor Dick leaned forward, pipe in hand, his eyes bright as blue steel in the lamp-glow.

"Now this isn't treating me on the level, old Mary." He waved his pipe in reproach. "You know very well the vicar and I are trying to rake up Troon's past history. I've been here for the last hour and you've never let out one solitary squeak."

"No, and I wouldn't have done it if Jim hadn't seen what he has seen this night." Her bright dark eyes flashed round the intent faces.

"I've been thinking over that business you've been telling about, Doctor Dick, that skeleton Joe dug out of the walls last week. Seems like as if that must have been her skeleton."

No one contradicted this dark surmise.

"I'll tell you the story as my grandfeyther's grandfeyther wrote it. He was a scholar. Kept village school up at Keston. He'd got an old book with everything put down that happened since Seagate began. I read this story when I was a girl and never forgot a word. I can get the book from my uncle's niece by marriage that works in a big library up to London to prove I'm right."

Chairs were hitched up, pipes relit. Old Tom flung a log that roused the fire to crackling flame. Solomon emerged, paced majestically back to his mistress, stretched at her feet with his yellow chin supported on them.

"The year 1600 saw Troon put up at the end of the parade, only a low seawall then. Course Troon was naught but a little tavern then: Troon Tavern. Even for those rough times it was a bad place. They had miners over from Flint across the water—dark little devils, those Welshmen, always scrapping and more handy with knives than a butcher himself. Mostly it was miners went to Troon Tavern. The man that built it was Thomas Werne, a Seagate man that got hold of money somehow. Smuggling, most like.

"Werne, the book said, was nothing but a block brute of a man.

Treated his young wife wors'n dog. When she died he got downright savage, and the child, Lizzy, left to him, came in for it all. I'm not going to harrow your feelings nor my own by telling what that innocent suffered. Laws weren't much then when it came to looking after poor people's children.

"But there was a gentleman came to stay here at this very inn, the Three Mariners, and he was that angry when he saw Lizzy and learned about her from Seagate talk, he threatened he'd have Werne put in prison. The gentleman went back to London after that and told Werne he'd hear more about it. Well, next thing that happened was—Lizzy Werne disappeared."

"Ah!" Doctor Dick's voice poignantly expressed his thought.

"Yes. Every one was certain sure Werne had done it, same as you're thinking yourself," responded old Mary. "But nothing could be proved. The body of the child, not much more of it than bones Joe found, never turned up, search though they might and did! The law made a great fuss when it was too late. The gentleman from London came back and he stayed for weeks, he was that set on getting Werne hanged for murder."

"And he walled the child up in his own house, then!" Doctor Dick's eyes blazed.

"Aye. After three hundred years we've found what Werne did, I b'lieve!"

"Eh, think of that!" Old Tom spat into the red fire. "And what did the murderin' fellow say had happened to the child? What did he tell 'em?"

"Said she was drowned. No one ever knew whether or not she was, the tides being mortal quick and dangerous here at Seagate. An' 'twas worse then. There were quicksands down by the marshes, and more than Werne's Lizzy had been caught and drowned. No one believed Werne's tale, only nothing could be done to him because Lizzy's body was never found."

"Quite. What I don't see," put in Doctor Dick, "is why he walled the body up. After smashing her skull, why not have taken the corpse out to sea and dropped it overboard one dark night?"

Old Mary shook her head.

"You mean he hadn't a boat?"

"No, I don't mean that, Doctor Dick. All the Seagate men had boats in those days, same as you and me have a pair of shoes. Reckon you're the only one here doesn't know why he couldn't put that body in the sea."

There were confirmatory nods all round the silent spellbound circle.

Doctor Dick frowned in bewilderment.

"Why?"

"Well, seeing you don't know, I'll say the verse that was in the old book my granfeyther's grandfeyther wrote out;

"A murdered body cast to sea
May never there lie quietly,
But every night is washed
    ashore,
And standing by the murderer's
    door
It cries to be let in.

"Of course that's put in rhyme and it's not quite right about the tides, not being a high tide every night anyhow. But the tide or no tide, the ghost would come back to the man who did the murder every night of his life."

Jim Sanderson shivered and looked with haunted eyes at the old woman.

"You reckon I saw her then—the ghost?"

"No. There's one, and it's a downright dangerous one. The child escaped, thanks be! But Werne's caught himself now and he's going to make people suffer for it."

She turned to Doctor Dick.

"That padlock you told me about, with the red marks on it. Magic that was, black magic to keep the child's soul a prisoner all these years. Sold her to the devil, did her father! Just so long as the child was promised, Werne himself was free."

Sanderson made an abrupt movement.

"I don't know as I get your meaning, old Mary."

"Plain enough. He'd sold his child to the devil, same as you'd bind an apprentice. The devil, he taught Werne how to lock her up safe so as her little ghost couldn't escape and go wandering round, making people suspect. Well, that spell was broken when Joe Dawlish broke down the wall and the padlock and chain."

"As far as that goes," Doctor Dick's crisp voice interrupted the old woman's uncomfortably clear exposition, "the vicar and I are equally to blame."

"And Werne's not going to forget it," warned old Mary. "Now Lizzie's bones lie in the churchyard all safe and sound there'll be trouble —black trouble. That's how I see it, anyways."

Jim sucked in his breath on a long tremulous hiss. The fishermen got to their feet.

"Reckon the tide's right enough now," said one.

"Wait! I'll come along." Jim lunged clumsily in the wake of the re-treating men. "You're going my road and I'll be glad of company tonight."

Old Mary's serious withdrawn look followed the group out. As the heavy outer door banged to, she shook her head.

"Jim Sanderson's in for it," she said in a low voice. "After sunset it's asking for trouble to set foot in Troon. He'll go like Joe Dawlish went. Poor fellow . . . poor fellow!"

The next afternoon, Troon stood in a blaze of sunlight. The sky was mother-of-pearl. A slow full tide gleamed like gray satin. Troon con-fronted it—cold, indifferent, implacable.

Inside its strong walls an army of workmen went about like busy scurrying ants. They were desperate to finish this job. Work that would ordinarily have lingered on for weeks was being rushed through at treble speed. One week more would see painting and decorations complete. Even the long wilderness of a garden was being dug and planted and trimmed and sown at a pace contrary to all Seagate tradition.

Doctor Dick lingered outside the strip of grass and iron rail pro-tecting Troon's tall front windows on the ground floor. Lynneth had told him she was coming with the Kinlochs about three o'clock this afternoon. Elaborate juggling with his day's appointments brought him to Troon on the stroke of the hour.

"Afternoon, doctor!"

A joiner called Frost touched his cap. He carried a big woven basket of tools over his shoulder. His face looked bleached. He glanced back over his shoulder as he stepped from Troon's front door and blinked in the clear light outside the house.

"Knocking off already?"

"Aye, sir. Not worth going to fetch more tools for half an hour."

Doctor Dick stared. Laughed.

"You don't mean your day finishes at three-thirty, Frost? I envy you."

"There's none of us works there," he jerked a backward thumb, "after three-thirty, sir. Not these short days. All on us goes at three-thirty—before dusk," he added with significance.

"I see. How do you square that up with regulations?"

"We begins at seven 'stead of eight o' mornings, sir. That's how we does it. The boss is agreeable so long as we does a regular day all told."

"Leave before sundown. Yes, I see."

"We've got good reasons for it."

"I believe you."

"Aye. Not a man would stay in Troon after dusk. No—not for a ransom, not since Jim Sanderson went. A cruel death! Went like Joe Dawlish—just the same."

Seeing the doctor's grave expression, Frost began speaking again.

"Mark my words, sir, if them two iggerant foreigners—if you'll excuse me putting it so bald-like—wot are renting the bungalow over by the marshes—"

"Mr. and Mrs. Kinloch?"

"Aye. If them two move into Troon next week, all I say is they'd do better to go down marsh-walk and be drowned comfortable. Might as well die natural deaths like! That's wot I says and wot I sticks to."

Doctor Dick took this with gratifying seriousness. He went to his car and fiddled about with it for a minute or so to gain time, then returned with a thought he appeared to have found under the car's hood.

"Look here, Frost! Believing in anything makes it real. If the Kinlochs have no faith at all in old Werne and his power to hurt them, well, perhaps he can not."

Frost poked his head forward like a turtle emerging from its shell.

"Noa," his north-country accent marked strong emotion, "I doan't hold wi' thot and thee doesn't neether, Doctor Dick! Thot oogly Thing a-grinnin' and a-murderin' there in the dark like, it's naught to it what we b'lieves! It just bides quiet—same as a beast or summat—and then—— "

The man's gesture, brawny fist smashing downward, was eloquent.

Other workmen began to emerge from Troon. They mounted a fleet of bicycles leaning up against the iron railing and made for home and tea. Doctor Dick frowned. Surely the Kinlochs wouldn't—yes. There they were.

"Good afternoon, Doctor Thornton. Oh, I mean Doctor Dick—it's so difficult to bring myself to say that. In town, of course, one's so much more formal. D'you remember Doctor de Tourville, Alice? Imagine if we'd called him Doctor Henry! Of course he was really a consultant. A very big man. A personal friend of ours."

Doctor Dick let Edith's flow gush right over his head. She'd thought out her speech carefully in order to make two distinct impressions; first as to his regretable lack of professional dignity, second as to the standing she and Alec had enjoyed in Liverpool. She saw him turn to Lynneth. His rising color she attributed to having got home with her two little stabs. It was always inconceivable to Edith that anyone could just ignore her. She gave them credit for ordinary intelligence.

"You're not—not going over the house so late?"

Doctor Dick had eyes and ears for Lynneth only. Alec, on his way to the front door, turned back and surveyed the doctor with a dull eye of one whose liver is perpetually ill-treated.

"So late!" he echoed. "Late for what? Was old Werne expecting us earlier?"

He burst into a high-pitched laugh, disconcerting in a man of his size. Doctor Dick's glance went to the windows of the house before which they stood. He thought he heard a louder, gruffer laugh within— a workman, perhaps. Yes, something dark passed one of the bedroom windows at that moment.

Edith ran forward to the front door, all girlish abandon to take up her husband's witty remark. She lifted the knocker and gave a smart rat-tat-tat.

"We'll ask him if he'll give us tea."

She cast a glassy brown look over the shoulder of her ponyskin coat. Alec, fumbling for his key, laughed again, louder and longer. Edith gave vent to a selection of well-rehearsed "outbursts of merriment." Doctor Dick, alert and listening with painful intentness now, was convinced he heard a hoarse, coarse echo within the walls of Troon. It must be a workman—and—yet—. As he stood there, wondering how on earth he was going to prevent Lynneth from following the two Kinlochs inside, a further shock assaulted his nerves. Alec was still clumsily rooting for his mislaid key.

The heavy front door swung silently, widely open without a touch.

Edith blinked, frowned, assumed a bright tone of playfulness.

"We are invited for tea!" she laughed. "I suppose the men didn't pull the door to. How careless! I shall report it tomorrow to the foreman. These country yokels! Oh, well, one must be patient, I suppose."

Alec followed his wife inside. Doctor Dick drew Lynneth back.

"Look here—no right to interfere with you and all that—but don't go in!"

Her eyes were fathomless, shining. In the golden dusk her vivid eager face had a transparent look, as if it were wrought glass, golden-tinted, exquisite, through which rare wine sparkled and bubbled and gleamed.

"I—but why do you ask that?"

"Because it's dangerous. It's deadly. Your cousins don't or won't believe anything against Troon. But I tell you the truth. The place is haunted. There's a devil in it."

She looked at him very straightly under the fine beautiful arch of her brows. She knew truth when she heard it. She trusted this man. More than trusted—much, much more than that. For a moment her whole heart responded. Her hands were gripped in his.

"Lynneth! Oh, my dear!" he breathed.

"But—but—" she stammered in surprise. "Is it like this—like this? To feel so sure, when only yesterday—"

The front door banged violently. For a second their startled eyes questioned each other. Then they rushed forward. They had no key. Doctor Dick plied the knocker. Lynneth ran back to the front of the house to peer through the long windows. She returned to Doctor Dick.

"It's all right. Alec's there. He's talking to Edith from the hall. She must be upstairs."

They looked together. Yes, Alec was there safe and sound. He seemed annoyed. Under the hanging unshaded light his face was unhealthily sallow and fretful. His head was flung back. He was talking to someone above, but no sound was audible to the watchers.

They felt a queer chill of apprehension. His side of the conversation seemed acrimonious, to judge by his expression. His frown became a sullen scowl. He turned from the stairway up which he'd been looking, jammed his hat down, stalked away. Next moment he came outside, leaving the front door open behind him.

"Too damned cold in there to hang about. Edith's as obstinate as—"

He scowled at them, pulled out a pipe, clamped strong yellow teeth on its stem, and began to fill the bowl. After a few puffs he relaxed. Recent and surprising discomfort urged him to speech.

"Chill on my liver or something," he vouchsafed, "Edith insisted—well, you know what she is!" He turned to the girl. "Today's plans included a visitation here," he jerked a thumb inelegantly. "No consideration for my health—must go over the place. Doesn't matter that the house reeks of gas or something. And colder than a tomb. Damn it all, if she must see it, she'll see it without my company!"

Lynneth stared. Never, no, never had she heard him come so near a criticism of his wife. Even when absent in the flesh, her mind ruled his, subjugated it to her opinions. He must be extraordinarily upset.

Inside Troon's heavy old walls, Edith went confidently to and fro, snapping on lights, snapping off lights, rubbing a finger on surfaces of wood, raising an eyebrow at a pile of tools and shavings in the middle of a bathroom floor, opening every door in order that air should circulate. The house seemed strangely stuffy, although windows and ventilators were all opened this mild day to dry up paint and varnish and new plaster. And how much colder it was indoors than out! A great golden sun flung a path of light across five miles of sea and sand. Its clear shining reached Troon's gray western face. Six tall west windows met the golden light—and repelled it.

"But how absurd!"

Edith stared about with indignation. Her high heels clicked smartly on woodblock floors as she tried another room. Her room, the room she meant to call her boudoir. The most perfectly preserved in the whole lovely house with its south and west windows, its beams, its old, old corner fireplace so laboriously restored.

"What have they been doing—idiots!" The toffee-brown eyes took on a glaze of anger. "I told them vita-glass in this room. Do they think they can fob off this gray clouded stuff on me? I'd make them come back and change it right away if I were in charge. I shall ring up the contractor tonight. The very idea! These country bumpkins—tiresome things!"

The windows darkened and darkened as she glared about her. So angry was she that a voice from the doorway behind did not startle her at all; it merely represented a person on whom she could vent her vicious mood.

At sight of the big hulking weatherbeaten figure in stained ragged jersey and sea-boots, she let fly:

"Your're not a workman here?"

The grizzled ugly head made a gesture of denial.

"I'm Mrs. Kinloch."

The man stared, unenlightened by the great news. He was like some great dark bull with his lowered head and bloodshot savage eyes. Edith caught sight of the trail of leaf-mold, mud and dust that marked the intruder's path across polished flooring beyond the doorway.

"Look at the mess you've made. How dare you come tramping about here? Who are you?"

"Thomas Werne."

"Werne! Werne! Why, that's the same name as some unpleasant old man who's supposed to have lived here centuries ago! The one there's such a silly fuss about."

The man appeared uninterested.

"Well! You can go away—at once! D'you hear? Don't imagine because you've the same name as that creature that you've a right of entry to these premises. Be off at once."

He regarded her with a fixed glare. Abruptly he burst into a loud long hoarse laugh. It echoed and re-echoed through the hollow rooms.

Edith drew up her thin person in disgust.

"Really!" She soliloquized without troubling to lower her voice. "Must be a half-wit. These fisherman are the limit. Unpleasant dirty animals. Phew! How dark it's getting. I wish I hadn't stayed after all."

Her glance took in the blank windows, frowned at them. It was almost like an eclipse of the sun, something so queer and sudden and unnatural was in the gloom that spread . . . and spread.

She looked beyond the burly figure in the doorway. An immense skylight was set in the roof above the staircase. When she'd come up only ten minutes ago, clear strong light had shone down. She remembered thinking how well the oak-grain of the steep old stairs showed up after treatment. Now, a wall of impenetrable darkness lay behind the intruder.

Secret inadmissable fear lent a barb to her tongue. Baffled, furious, uncertain, she tried to assume the glacial manner of an aristocrat as she conceived one.

"I don't wish to get you into trouble, my good man, but unless you go—at once—I shall feel it my duty to report you to the police."

A noisy bellow answered her. "Report old Tom Werne, eh! Thot's a good 'un—a reet down dom good 'un!"

His great bulk shook like a jelly. Walls and floor and windows—the whole structure of old Troon seemed to strain and shake and quiver with its uncontrolable amusement.

She stamped her high-heeled shoe, so neat and polished.

"Oh, how dare you! Impertinent—I shall send Mr. Kinloch back to speak to you."

She took a few steps in the gray gloom toward the darker gloom outside, and stopped short. Raging inwardly, she was forced to realize that she couldn't, she positively couldn't make up her mind to go nearer that unpleasant filthy chuckling old beast in the doorway. Should she throw up a window and call to Alec? It would put her in a perfectly idiotic light. Infuriating impasse! She hesitated, summoned her reserves.

"I shall certainly give you in charge," she began. "The moment I—I—"

She blinked, stuttered. Was she mad, or blind, or ill?

Through the windows, golden sun streamed in across the floor, long gleaming ladders of light upon the beautiful wood. The landing outside shone in a yellow haze of cross-lights from open doors on every side. The doorway was empty before her. Empty! The flooring beyond was bare of every trace of dust or leaves.

She stood shivering, spellbound in the quiet sunset glow. Downstairs a door banged like a gun going off. Heavy feet resounded on the redbrick yard at the side of the house. They echoed, died away, swallowed up in the green shadowy depths of the long garden beyond.

Released from a spell, she ran downstairs, out the front door, and pulled it after her with an angry bang. She poured out to the waiting three her recent experience. Gesture and phrasing harked back to pre-Lady Bountiful days. Doctor Dick recognized hysteria. Lynneth recognized that sub-Edith she'd always felt but never heard before. Alec did not recognize anything. He regarded her with mulish lack-luster eye.

"You would go over the house! You are so damned obstinate! Must have been old Werne himself you were up there chatting to."

Edith's laugh rose shrill in the cool winter dusk.

"I can believe the doctor might say a thing like that. But you, Alec! Really! What are we coming to!"

"That's what I think. Old Werne himself. I've changed my mind since I went in just now. Not been in such a funk since I was a kid."

"So you left me to face it!"

"I did not. You did all the leaving part. Skipped up the stairs and left me cold. And cold's the word, too. I told you not to go. I knew something beastly was prowling around. Damn it all, you've got nerves of chromium-plated steel."

"Alec! How can you be so silly and so vulgar! Actually using language—in the public street—and to your own wife!"

The shock of it pulled her together quite effectually. She shot across the wide road and began to canter homeward. Alec turned to the doctor and grinned, a shamefaced but quite a human friendly grin.

"See you again, my boy. Looks as if you'd be needed at Troon to give us all nerve tonics and soothing-powders. Well—so long!"

He looked down at Lynneth. One of his more perceptive moments dawned.

"Better get a spot of walk after that scene, my child. I'll toddle home and see to Edith."

He lumbered off, a burly blot of all-British respectability against a sheet of silver water. Doctor Dick turned, eager, ready to make the most of every precious moment. The girl was standing with flower-like face entranced, lips parted, her whole attention absorbed.

"Lynneth! Lynneth darling! What are you looking at inside that horrible old house?"

She did not reply, did not seem to hear. She stood as in a dream, her hands gripping the pointed arrowheads that tipped the iron railing.

"What on earth—?"

He went to her side and peered in through dark blank panes of glass to Troon's lower floor. Darkness. Shadowy darkness.

Chill touched the leaping flame of joy in his heart. He put a hand on hers. She did not move.

"Lynneth! Lynneth!"

The shining of a street lamp showed her face clearly. It was smiling in happy wonder. She seemed intent on some marvel, some vision beyond the big blank windowpanes.

He hesitated. Short of force he couldn't wrench away those small hands that clutched the iron railing. He put an arm about her shoulders, tried to draw her to him, but she did not yield an inch. Her slim soft body might have been one of the iron uprights of the railing. Her eyes didn't flicker from their rapt gaze.

He made up his mind, put out his arms to exert full force, to drag her from Troon, from whatever she saw inside its haunted wall. Abruptly she sighed, loosed her grip, her eyes faded to disappointment, to sick misery.

"Oh, it's gone! The lovely, lovely thing! I can't tell you how lovely. But it's gone. It won't come back. Not now. But I'll watch for it again. I must see it soon again."

The man froze. His blood turned to ice. What deadly perilous thing had she seen? A trap—a snare had been set. For Lynneth—for Lynneth! Oh, God!

To all his anguished questioning she shook her head. Her eyes were sad, full of longing. Remote, distraught, she walked beside him.

"There are no words for it. I can't tell, even if I would. Clouds . . . clouds . . . and a new lovely world. I must go back there—go back—"

He shivered. A devil's trick. Old Werne had played a devil's trick to get her fast. She'd been afraid before. She would have been on guard. Now she only longed to be inside that cursed place, dreamed of it as a wanderer dreams of home.

Their precious hour together was a grim ordeal to him. She, withdrawn and silent, he sick with fear for her. And the end of the nightmare walk was as strange as any of it.

At the black and white gate of Sandilands the two took formal farewell. A rising moon lighted the dark road. On one side of it crouched the little bungalow, looking like a child's toy with its gables, and its fir-trees on either side of the straight formal garden-path. Opposite the odd little dwelling stretched a long meadow. Beyond lay half-drowned marshes—beyond them sand and shining pools left by the tide where seabirds clamored in the moonlight.

Doctor Dick strode away from the gate. He hadn't dreamed such black despair was possible. A voice called him.

"Dick! Dick! I want you. Come back!"

Next moment he had her in his arms. So close, so safe against his heart, it seemed nothing could hurt her again. She put him away at last, laughing, tears gleaming in her eyes.

"What happened to you—darling—darling?" she whispered. "I feel as if I'd waked from a nightmare. Kiss me! Again! Oh, Dick, you do care after all!"

II

"There now, Doctor Dick! Sit down and make yourself at home. It's a week since you've been in. What's worrying you, sir? Tom—a glass of sherry for the doctor."

The host, in blue striped shirtsleeves, apron girt about his beaver waistcoat, clattered off across the red-tiled room. Mrs. Burden looked with keen old eyes at her guest's shadowed face.

"Nothing wrong, so far?"

"No."

His monosyllable dropped like a stone into a deep well. "Nothing And it's unbearable. The suspense. Waiting—waiting—"

He sprang up, paced to and fro in the leaping firelight, stopped before the quiet watchful old woman, his hands clasped behind his back, legs astride, head thrust forward. She met his searching look and answered his agonized unspoken question in her unhurried fashion.

"Aye. There is danger for the lass every hour she's there. But there's just a gleam of hope to my mind, too."

"For Lynneth! You think so? Why, Mary?"

"That great dark Thing at Troon seems as if it settles on one at a time."

He frowned, stared.

"Then, if so—if so it's Mrs. Kinloch who's in the line of fire. I told you that she saw him—old Werne—and insists he was a drunken fisherman."

Old Mary was emphatic. "It was him. He came with the darkness that's part of him."

"Yes. Mrs. Kinloch admitted the darkness—at first. Went back on it later, though. Said she'd only imagined it got dark."

"She saw Werne. It's my belief she'll go next. Then you can take your lass away."

"But, good heavens! D'you mean I'm to wait until that devil murders Mrs. Kinloch?"

"What other way is there?"

Her calm matter-of-factness roused in him a sudden hysterical desire to roar with laughter. And after all, he had to wait! If that obstinate woman—

"I've asked her a dozen times to leave Troon. She's on the point of forbidding me the house," he admitted.

"Waste no more words," advised the old woman. "They'll take you nowhere. Your job is to save the lass. Never mind fretting over them as are blind and deaf as stones.''

Old Tom returned and poured the wine. Doctor Dick sat down, glass in hand.

"How about the servant lassies at Troon?" asked Mr. Burden.

"From Liverpool," the doctor said. "They've heard nothing so far, Dressed up town girls, too superior to be friendly with Seagate fishermen. They've only one complaint so far."

"Aye!"

"They say Troon's dark. Grumble about the windows—that the glass is always gray and clouded even when the sun's shining outside."

"Darkness. 'Thing of Darkness'—that's what parson called it the day he buried Joe Dawlish."

"Thing of Darkness." Doctor Dick rose. His face was drawn and stern. "Well, I must be off. I'm dining at Troon. A housewarming. I'll call in again after it's over. It's likely to be a housewarming that leaves me cold."

The heavy door clanged behind him.

"He'll not come back this night." Mrs. Burden turned a solemn face to her husband. He sat in his favorite chair, drawing on his churchwarden. "Friday, 'tis! And full moon. And—I didn't tell Doctor Dick purposely—he's enough on his mind—but it's the anniversary of the day Lizzie Werne disappeared. It's written in that old book I told you of. December 2nd, 1636."

"You think old Werne'll—?"

"Aye. I think he will."

"You must excuse this picnic meal." Edith's eyes were ablaze with triumph. Hard bright color dyed her thin cheeks. "I warned you it would be a case of roughing it. The maids have done their best, but you know what they are!"

Four sat at the gate-legged table of Jacobean oak for dinner that night, the seventh night of the Kinloch's arrival at Troon. Edith had worked like a beaver, had driven cook and housemaid before her whirl of energy like galley-slaves. The big gaunt house was furnished from wide shadowy attics to scrubbed and scoured kitchens and pantries.

Doctor Dick remembered the Biblical story of the man possessed of a devil, who swept and garnished his house. He remembered and shivered.

He made the reply his hostess expected of him. The well-pointed table, the gleaming silver and dinnerservice chosen to harmonize with the house, the five-course dinner, the well-trained maids imported from town, were all elaborate and overemphatic in perfection. Not the natural and dignified background of a wellbred hostess, but a show. Herself the blatant complacent showman!

"Alone I did it," her voice, manner, and conversation implied.

"You know," she reproached the visitor, "I really believe you're disappointed. I think I see—yes, I'm sure I do—a sort of 'I'd rather that my friend should die than my prediction prove a lie' expression on your face."

Alec intervened. He, at least, had the advantage of early discipline that had planted certain fixed rules of conduct in him. Doctor Dick looked ill at ease. He must be soothed. Hang it all, you didn't rub things in at your own dinner-table! Edith was a bit above herself to-night. She'd got her way. They were living at Troon. Things were all right too—at least—He brushed away suspicion. Just an effect of lighting. He wasn't used to the queer old house yet.

"Noticed the fireplace?" he asked. "It's part of the original tavern. Sort of bakehouse. The whole inglenook, arches and chimney breast and the little iron door to shove ashes through, were covered up by a kitchen range. Lovely old stuff that brick—three hundred years old."

Thankfully, the guest accepted the diversion.

"Makes a wonderful dining room. That window too, I like the square panes—different from the silly imitations they make. Set in that battered old framework it's—hello! Who's that looking in? D'you keep a gardener working at this hour?"

Edith glanced up quickly, wished she'd drawn the curtains after all. She'd decided, on such a romantic moonlight night, that the vista of garden enhanced the room's perfection. Impatiently she tinkled a small copper bell at her hand. No one answered it. She rang again, waited. No sound from outside.

Lynneth ventured a suggestion. She was in one of the strange dreamy moods that the doctor dreaded—moods that had recurred again and again since that night of her "vision," as she called it. Her dinner-gown of smoke-gray velvet with its gleam of gold thread, the jewel—Tiger's Tear—glinting tawny-yellow on her breast, the thick shining hair like folded wings about her head, all gave Doctor Dick a pang of terror and dismay. She looked unreal tonight, held in dreams, unaware of evil, of danger coming stealthily nearer as she slept.

"I think," the girl's voice was only a whisper, "I think they've gone away. Someone—came for them."

Edith's answer was sharp with vexation. "My dear girl, what an idea! Go away in the middle of my dinner party? Why? They don't know a soul here. Really, Lynneth! You look half asleep. You'd better go and look for them. It might rouse you."

Doctor Dick sprang to his feet. "No. Let me go, please!"

Edith raised resigned exasperated brows. He would behave like this. How irritating these unconventional people were! He seemed to think this was a picnic, after all. Taken her literally. So stupid! Spoiling the whole tone of her dinner. Now they'd all have to get up. She and Alec couldn't sit still and let a guest chase about the house.

She rose, stood with finger-tips on the table, lifted her chin, looked around from under lowered lids in what she knew to be a really compelling pose. Her Queen Elizabeth look, she termed it privately. More privately still, she was sure there was some strain of royal blood in her. Some ancestor of hers had been—er—naughty! Oh, she was sure. How else did she come by the profound conviction of her own superiority? She knew she was different—an aristocrat deep down.

"I will go myself," she pronounced. "I insist. The maids are my province, after all."

Lynneth was unmoved by majesty's withdrawal. She seemed to be listening to some far-off entrancing sound. The two men looked uncertainly at each other. Alec assumed a boisterous hearty manner.

"Drink up, drink up! Fill your glass, my boy, and pass the claret along. The girls are new to Seagate. Heard something and dashed out to investigate, I expect. You know how pin-headed they are."

Minutes passed. No sound from hall or kitchens. Then came the tap-tap of high heels just overhead.

"Edith! Girls must've gone upstairs, not outside. I wonder—"

"We ought to go up, too."

Doctor Dick was on his feet. Alec, puzzled and uncomfortably disturbed by something he did not begin to understand, rose also. They made for the door. The doctor turned back, to see Lynneth sitting peacefully at the table, dreaming, indifferent.

"Stay there. Don't move from this room," he called back. "Lynneth! Lynneth!"

She responded with a vague absent smile. Doctor Dick followed his host with a last anxious look of love at the girl. A sense of mortal deadly peril threatened. The whole house seemed growing dark and suffocating and evil.

A cry came from above. Every light dimmed, went out. Thick choking darkness muffled Troon from kitchens to attics. Blindly, Doctor Dick fought his way up.

"Where are you?" he called.

From the stairs above, he heard Alec's voice, muffled, cursing.

"What's wrong? What are you doing? Can't you answer me, man?"

"I'm trying—to—get down."

Alec's voice came thicker, fainter now. A stumble. Curses and sound of hoarse hurried breathing in the darkness above. Then there was a yell—the crack of splintering wood—a heavy body came slithering and sprawling down the stairs as if flung with immense force. It knocked against Doctor Dick as he was stumbling upward, and he fell too, slipping down until an angle in the wall stopped him. Winded, uninjured, uncertain what to do next, he called out.

"Lynneth! Lynneth! Are you all right? Can you find matches? I left my lighter in my overcoat."

No answer from the profound d. kness below.

"Lynneth!"

A voice, a vague faint echo of the girl's clear tone, floated down from above, it seemed to him. He made his way up the steep narrow old stairs again. "Lynneth! Lynneth!"

Edith Kinloch, cinnamon-brown silk flounces rustling her indignation, pursued her search. The kitchens, the pantries, were ablaze with light. And the hall.. And the landing upstairs. She looked quickly into the rooms on the ground floor. No one there. But every room was brilliantly lighted.

She stamped her annoyance. Was this some low silly joke? Had the two maids gone off for some reason, leaving on all the lights merely to upset her? But why? Why? There had been no trouble over anything. Later perhaps, when they knew she did not intend to get more help—

She ran upstairs. Here again all lights were on. Every bedroom door was flung widely open. The blood rose to her head. In a rage now, she went up the last steep twisting staircase to the attics, and once more found the same silly prank had been played. True the lights were less brilliant. Fifteens were good enough for maids to waste! They'd only read in bed and be late in the morning if she gave them stronger lamps.

She hadn't thought fifteens were quite so poor though. Why, one candle would give more light than these things. Must be faulty bulbs. She'd ring up and complain tomorrow. They seemed to be getting dimmer as she looked at them. One died right out overhead. The one over the stairwell. She'd turn her ankle getting down again.

But where were those fools of girls? She stalked across to the wardrobe. There hung the tweed coats they wore, and a lot of other clothes. They couldn't have run off. They must be in the garden. She'd go down and send Alec out to find them.

Lynneth would have to make coffee and serve it, to cover the gap. Thank heaven, they'd finished the last course, anyhow. She turned about on the square landing, a mere three-foot platform, from which the attics opened.

In the big west room a sound brought her head about with a jerk. "Who's there? Is that you, Beasley? Parkes?"

A shuffle. A heavy tread. She went back to the room. A light clicked off in the room as she entered it. She wheeled with a little squeal of anger.

"How dare you—"

In the darkness, a blacker deadlier darkness moved. Held rigid in sudden cold fear, her eyes accustomed themselves to the gloom. The window stood widely open. No. Not open. She looked at the thing. No window or even frame was there. Merely a ruinous irregular break in the crumbling wall.

She went to it, dizzy, sick, her nostrils filled with dusty choking stench. Her eyes followed the swelling shapeless Thing of Darkness that moved in the moonlit darkness of the room. A sudden red light shone from a foul little lantern that stood on a stone shelf formed by the chimney-breast's irregularities. Bare crumbling brick, the chimney was.

"But this"—she spoke aloud in a hoarse amazed voice—"this is what it was before we restored it. This isn't our Troon!"

"No. It's mine."

Loud voice and louder laughter answered her. She recognized them. In the smoking lamplight, she saw the vast ugly bulk, the bloated face, the small cruel eyes set under matted hair.

"You! You here again! I thought I told you—"

Her voice died. Her cold hands flew to her throat. She pressed back —back against the dirty old wall behind. The other attic was darkened now; her frightened eyes glanced across to it. She was up here in the dark, shut up with this brutal mad old man. It was a trick! Those servants! She'd have them punished. A monstrous experience! How dare they let her be subjected to it!

Ah!—he was moving nearer—nearer—darkness, thick black choking darkness, rolled forward like a tidal wave.

Now it touched her. She shrieked. Ice-cold, wet, like rotting slime, it touched her—closer about her—closer! Backward she went before the stifling death—back to the gaping ruinous wall. If she could get to that —call for help! Yes! Yes! She was on her knees on the dusty uneven broken flooring. With desperate effort she twisted, thrust her head outside.

"Help! Help!" she shrieked. "Help!"

The word choked in her throat. She was drawn back, as if the room were a quicksand into which she sank—down—down—silken flounces ripped—hair fallen all about her face of idiot terror—down—down— through the door of life—down through hell's dark gates—down—down —the Thing of Darkness pressed closer—closer still . . . .

It seemed to Doctor Dick, fighting his way in the unnatural darkness, as if he struggled up through clouds of poisonous gas whose fumes took strength from his limbs, sight from his eyes. Gasping. Dragging himself up one stair at a time. A cold numbness invaded him.

Then a frightful bubbling shriek pierced his senses. It came from above. Another—and more horrible cry. He groaned. He couldn't hurry. He felt consciousness being blotted out. Darkness pressed on him like solid walls. A stench of rotted decay filled his nostrils, choked the breath in his throat . . . it failed him . . . he fell forward.

Darkness flowed over him like the river of death itself.

He opened his eyes to find himself lying on the stairs just below the first-floor landing. Electric lights winked on all sides. Gray dawn met his aching bewildered eyes through a vast skylight overhead.

He tried to think, to remember as he struggled to rise. How had he come there? Why did such heavy desperate weariness weigh him down?

Sick, trembling with effort, he stood clinging to the baluster rail. Below, under the glare of a droplight, he caught sight of a man sprawled untidily across a glowing Persian rug. Groaning, he stumbled down to investigate.

It was Alec who lay there. Doctor Dick's professional instinct pricked him from lethargy as he examined the man. "Broken leg, slight concussion," he murmured. Suddenly full recollection flashed in his clouded mind.

"Lynneth! Lynneth!" he called aloud.

He made for the dining-room where he had left her last night. The place was deserted. Lights gleamed dismally in the half daylight. The dinner-table's bravery of silver and glass mocked his distraught gaze. He searched the lower rooms. No one.

He passed Alec as if he'd been part of the hall furniture, and went upstairs. Lights burned everywhere. The air was chill but clean. Empty room after empty room greeted him vacantly. Only the last narrow stairs now to the wide attics above.

"Lynneth!"

He sprang up the topmost flight, and crouched beside the crumpled heap of gray velvet.

Her dark head was against the wall, blood stained her face, her soft white neck, the bosom of her dress. The Tiger's Tear had fallen back against her parted lips—gleaming golden bauble.

Wild meaningless phrases shot into his distraught mind. Bits of Ecclesiastes: "The silver cord is loosed . . . the golden bowl—"

He touched her, bent closer. Ah, it was not death after all! Not death. He was all physician now. The healer. Dare he lift her to examine further? That headwound was very deep—blood still welling. His eyes grew cold with fear once more as he explored it. The skull was crushed at one place. How could he move her from that awkward corner? It would be fatal to jolt her wounded head.

He hesitated only a moment. He must do it, of course. He daren't leave her alone in Troon while he got help. And every second counted. If ever he thanked heaven for his strength, it was now. When, with infinite care he'd laid her down at last on a bed in the nearest room on the floor below the attics, he went to the bathroom.

From an elaborately fitted-out medicine chest there, on which Edith had greatly plumed herself, he dug out what he could. Gray dawn brightened to day as he fought to save Lynneth. He used what makeshift medicaments he had. Dark hair he'd cut away was strewn on a pale costly rug beside the bed. The girl's face looked carved from frozen snow beneath its bandages. Her pulse beat ominously beneath his touch.

Her life hung balanced by a thread, and he watched with increasing fear. She must lie undistrubed now for another twenty-four hours at least. There was a slim, a very slim chance of life—no chance at all if she moved.

But there was another night to face—another night at Troon. How could he protect her? What weapons could a man use against the Thing of Darkness? Brooding, pondering, dazed with the terrific strain of the past hours, he sat. A creaking sound startled him.

It was Mrs. Burden. She was coming upstairs. He took her hands, kissed her withered cheek, tears of relief in his eyes at the sight of the old woman's calm face and faithful eyes.

"You're a miracle. No one in the world but you would have come. Now perhaps—"

He poured out in brief hurried whispers what he'd seen and heard last night.

"Servants gone. Kinloch's smashed up. Edith Kinloch's gone. I couldn't look for her. I daren't leave Lynneth alone for a minute in this house."

"Best look now, sir. I'll bide with your lass."

She settled down beside the patient like a little brown bird, watching the unconscious girl, taking in the room with clear thoughtful old eyes.

Doctor Dick went upstairs to begin his search. She heard him coming slowly down at last; heard his heavy breathing as if he carried some awkward weight. He had to pass the open door of the room where she sat. She saw what it was he carried.

Its broken neck revealed what once had been a human face—now a darkened dreadful mask. A few tattered wisps of silk clung to the broken body. Jeweled rings glittered on limp and dusty hands.

Doctor Dick passed on, went into a room near by. When he came in to her again he looked like an old man.

"You saw—it?"

Mrs Burden nodded solemnly.

"Wait here, sir. Coffee laced with brandy is what you need. We'll talk when you're better, my lamb—sir, I mean—begging your pardon!"

"Wait!" His hoarse voice detained her. "There's Kinloch, poor chap! Help me lift him. I don't think he's seriously hurt.

"There's no way out. We've got to spend this coming night at Troon. The chances are we'll go"—Doctor Dick made a gesture to the bedroom across the landing—"like . . . that!"

"No. Not like that. Whatever comes, not like that. It's true, as you said, 'tis no good letting any other body come inside this place. 'Tis for you and me—this night's work. No one else can help. Even the vicar himself couldn't. 'Tis for you and me. But no one of us will go—the way she did! No. If we have to die, I can take the three of us an easier road than that."

Day faded. Its last gold shone above the distant hills. A gleaming path lay across the water. The gold dimmed, and died. Darkness began to fall. Shadows thickened within the walls of Troon.

Mrs. Burden got up from her chair, beckoned the doctor to the door of Lynneth's room.

"You must leave things to me from this hour on. Keep your door fast bolted inside. Don't open it, not even if you think you hear my own voice call. 'Twould be a trick of old Werne that—to get you out of here. For God's sake, Doctor Dick, heed what I'm telling you. Stay inside until daylight comes. Bide with your lass here, if you want her to live, and want to live yourself."

"If you'd only tell me what you're up to, Mary! It's horrible to shut you out, to leave you alone—with that devilish thing."

"Eh, haven't we talked enough o' that? All the day long you've argued wi' me, Doctor Dick, and I tell you mind's made up. I'm old, too old to fear death. And I know things—things I can't tell you, sir. Bolt the door—and leave it fast till daylight."

Moving with sure unhurried purpose outside the bolted door, Mrs. Burden went to and fro among the shifting looming shadows. She had all prepared. She made no mistake.

There was only one way to shut out a damned soul. The cross itself. A cross of living flesh and blood.

In the wood-frame of the door, outside, four great hooks had been screwed in by Doctor Dick that day. Iron hooks that Mrs. Burden had brought prepared for her purpose, two at the top corners of the cross-piece, and one on either side of the door. From these hooks she hung four plaited loops of hair and hempen rope—two long loops from the top, two very short ones on either side.

She stood with back against door and slipped the long right-hand loop beneath her left armpit, and the long left-hand loop beneath her right armpit. Then, supported so that fatigue should not make her fall, she thrust her hands through the small handcuff loops on either side to keep her arms straight out from her body.

So she stood, a small light bird-like figure. Through the big roof-window, glimmering stars and rising moon showed her in the dusk, a human crucifix past which the Thing of Darkness might not go.

Facing Troon and its evil. Frail old body. Staunch old soul.

Daylight. Daylight and Lynneth had passed the crisis! She was safe. Doctor Dick opened the door. The light worn body of Old Mary hung there still.

It was an empty shrine, too old, too tired to survive the night's long vigil and shock of battle—an empty shrine, but not marred, not touched by hurt or evil. The Thing of Darkness had left no shadow in the calm sightless eyes, no lines of terror or dismay on the peaceful worn face; only deep exhaustion. A victor fallen at the goal.

A victor. Yes, Doctor Dick knew that. For long minutes he looked at the frail triumphant figure, assurance of her victory deep in his heart; giving homage to the dead, giving thanks for her divine courage.

His eyes, blinded with tears, lifted to see something else at last. A hulking black-haired man stood against an opposite wall. As the doctor stared, red sunrise dyed the skylight window above, touched the ugly brutal figure with flame.

It shrank, quivered. Its purple lips opened in soundless rage. Its dark bulk glowed like molten metal. White-hot . . . sullen red . . . dissolving . . . writhing . . . twisting in the sun's merciless fire to inhuman appalling decay—to a rag and wisp of a thing—to a shriveled black mummy that grinned in age-old death.

That too dissolved and was split like sand and running through an hourglass. It lay on the jade-green Chinese carpet, a drift of gray dust, last grim symbol of mortality.

The shadow-life that Werne had bargained for was finished. Soul, will, poisonous hate were blotted out. The blackest magic could perpetuate his borrowed existence no longer. The deepest hell could offer no shelter for his furious ghost. Werne—Thing of Darkness—was no more.

But the old house still fronts sea and sky hills. Troon—old Troon. Shell of death. Desolate. Betrayed.

One of the most popular stories ever to appear in WEIRD TALES was a short-short story entitled "Three Marked Pennies" by Mary Elizabeth Counselman. While that story has been reprinted numerous times, more than two dozen other Counselman stories in WEIRD TALES have remained ignored by anthologists. Hopefully, the reprinting of this strange tale of murder and madness, one of Ms. Counselman's best tales, will encourage further revival of her work.

THE ACCURSED ISLE

Mary Elizabeth Counselman

Landers drove another sliver of shell into the rotting log. The other six men watched with listless eyes, while Clark counted soundlessly.

"Fifteen," he finished aloud. "Fifteen days since the liner went down. Lord! We've been on this God-forsaken island only two weeks! It seems like fifteen years at least since I ate a good square meal. Mm . . . I think I'd give my corner lot in hell for a rare steak . . . with onions," he said dreamily. "And a pile of French fried potatoes as high as my head!"

"Shut up!" snapped Ellis savagely, scowling at the speaker. "Don't make it no worse than it is!"

They huddled together on the white sand, seven men who would find nothing in common back there in New York, but who were welded together now to cheat their mutual foe—Death. Seven pairs of eyes stared out across the endless expanse of green-blue water to where the sun was just dipping into the sea. Landers glanced about at the group pensively. He had grown to know them well, these companions of his, during those interminable fifteen days. In that mad chaos when the ship went down, the instinct to live had tumbled them into the little lifeboat and put out from the steamer, wallowing heavily in the angry sea. Many were lost, but the rescue freighter that cabled its nearness must have picked up most of the loaded boats. But one remained unaccounted for, Landers pondered bitterly, a boat containing seven men. They had tossed all that terrible night, with Death snatching at them from every towering billow, and when morning came, the boat thumped against a jutting knoll of reef—a bare twenty feet wide, but land. They had scrambled joyously from their leaky craft to cling to the knoll, and as the sun rose higher, the tide receded to reveal a small island about a square mile in area. Floating timbers and dead fish lay upon the sloping beach, and beyond in the soft mud, they found a supply of food—oysters. So they waited, drinking sparingly from their two meager kegs of water and subsisting on the shell-fish; confidently at first, then hopefully, then desperately at last.

By day a flag made from their shirts flapped from the peak of the knoll to beckon chance passing ships to the rescue. By night a small signal-fire burned, fed cautiously by the driftwood salvaged from the beach when the tide went out. At the tide's lowest ebb, the seven burrowed in the soft mud for shell-fish, which they piled about the signal flag, and when the sea rose to cover all save that little knoll, they clung there together till the tide went out.

But seven men, Landers mused, can not live indefinitely on the water in two small kegs, with shell-fish as their sole item of diet. The strain was telling on them all, and each marveled at the others' efforts not to show it. Landers stared covertly at each familiar face in the fading light. There was Ogden, a bluff and good-natured riveter whose winning of a fabulous sum at the big race in Agua Caliente had sent him abroad to satisfy his longing for travel. There was Ellis, sour and petty and illiterate old Texan, whose tiny farm had miraculously spouted oil one day. There was Anderson, likable but secretive, a boy of nineteen with a hunted look that betrayed something of his reason for leaving America. There was Kenshaw, a quiet and cheerfully courageous man of middle age, a doctor bound for the Orient to experiment with Mongol fevers. There was Ritters, as short of temper as he was of stature, by his own admission "the Big Guy's bodyguard"—the "Big Guy" being the notorious beer-baron who had probably escaped in another lifeboat. There was Clark, placid and unmoved in the face of their creeping peril, a globetrotter with an unquenchable desire to move on and a large enough inheritance to do so. And there was himself, Martin Landers, sent abroad by his firm to straighten out their Paris branch before he could return to—or send for, according to the time needed for adjustment—his wife and little son.

Oh, they all had their cherished little plans, Landers pondered bitterly—plans so effectively smashed when that fire in the liner's hold had broken out. He sighed and tossed a used match to the signal-fire, with a glance of revulsion at the heap of oysters about the signal flag.

"The night cometh . . . " murmured Doctor Kenshaw.

"Yeah," said Ogden. "Another night."

"Time to put on the nose-bag," spoke up the diminutive Ritters bitterly. "Pass the pocket-knife, Landers."

Landers tendered the short blade to the speaker. Ritters took it, muttering, and began to pry open one after another of the oyster shells. He tendered one ironically to the doctor. Kenshaw turned his head away with a grimace of repugnance.

"Oh, come, doctor!" sneered the gunman. "The sea-food at our joint is the best in town!"

Ogden spat disgustedly.

"Better take it, sir," the quiet boy at Kenshaw's left urged. "Have to eat . . . something, you know."

The doctor nodded slowly and forced himself to swallow the mollusk, gagging as he did so.

"None for me!" said Ellis vehemently. "Think I'd rather starve, if it's the same to you." He glowered at Landers sullenly. Landers returned the look with the dislike of a good sport for a squawker.

"I still think we oughta try for it," Ellis grumbled. "We must be just off the track of the steamers, and we're sure to run into one sooner or later. Why stick here on this rotten two-by-four island?"

"You know it would be suicide, Ellis," Landers said without emotion. "The boat sprang a slow leak when we hit the reef. But even if we could plug it up, it would mean leaving our food supply. And how can we know how soon a ship—"

"Well, our water supply is gettin' low," reminded the Texan ominously. "If we ain't picked up soon—"

"Aw, go to sleep!" growled Clark, who was already stretched out on the rocks beyond the tide line. "Who's the sentry tonight?"

"I am," replied Anderson hesitantly. "First half, that is, and Ogden relieves me."

"Well, mind you don't go to sleep on us like you done last time," Ellis turned his ill-feeling on the youth. "Like as not you let a ship pass."

The boy's face in the flickering firelight looked distressed.

"Aw, pipe down!" growled Ogden. "The kid's a bare nineteen—he couldn't help fallin' asleep." He yawned noisily, flopped on the sand, and closed his eyes. In a moment he was asleep like a healthy animal.

At length all of them sprawled about the small fire, far enough away to escape its heat in the sultry night, yet near enough to be out of the water when the tide rose. Only Anderson sat up, staring into the dark. There was no sound save the lapping of the waves on the beach, the intermittent crackle of the fire, the heavy breathing of the sleepers. The boy strained to pierce the blackness ahead, scanned the unseen waters for a glimpse of a passing ship, but only the distant stars met his roving gaze.

The lapping of the waves was infinitely soothing. Anderson nodded, jerked awake, nodded again. He rose once to pile more wood on the drying fire, sat back down and dozed once more. Once a muffled gasping sound started him from sleep, but he reminded himself that it could only be one of his companions having a nightmare. His head sank slowly upon his chest. The next he knew, Ogden's kindly face bent above him tolerantly, bidding him to lie down and sleep. The youth curled up where he sat and slept at once.

Excited voices roused him, and someone shaking him violently. His waking thought was that a ship had seen their signal-fire; but Ogden's face, bent above him, held no elation—rather a fixed horror.

"It's Ellis!" he rasped. "He's dead. Something slipped up on him in the night and . . . and tore out his throat," he finished in a rush of words.

The men were surrounding something that lay just beyond the water's edge in the dim gray light of dawn. Clark whistled soundlessly, looked away. Kenshaw was kneeling, examining the still form for any remaining signs of life.

"He's done for," he reported quietly. Landers was bending over the body also, and as Kenshaw looked up, their eyes met and held significantly.

"Some sea-monster, I guess," the doctor added rapidly. "Anybody know the funeral service?"

No one did.

"Well, we'll have to bury him anyway . . . out here." He gestured toward the open sea. "Some of you bail out the boat so we can row out a piece . . . ."

When they rowed back from the makeshift burial at sea, the little island had grown. They made the boat fast and threw themselves on the wet sand. No one spoke. They merely sat there, silent and shaken, until the tide ebbed. The task of gathering driftwood and delving for oysters broke the spell at last, however, and they spoke again in natural tones.

The day crept by at a maddening pace, and it was night again.

"My watch, isn't it?" Landers spoke, driving another sliver of shell into the log. "Clark, you're my relief." Clark nodded, swallowing an oyster, with a wry face.

They curled up at last and slept. Landers squatted beside the fire, staring out into the dark and praying in his unpracticed way for that precious blaze of light that would be a rocket from a passing ship. Once he thought he heard a movement behind him in the darkness. He tried to peer into the engulfing shadow beyond the aura from the fire. A swishing sound came from the other side of the island.

Landers stood up and took a step in that direction, but there was nothing to see, and the sound did not come again. He sat back down heavily, with a shrug of his square shoulders.

"Couldn't have been, " he muttered half aloud. "I'm crazy . . . but . . . Kenshaw noticed it too . . . aw, we're both crazy!"

Landers had learned to mark the hour by the creeping of the tide up the sloping beach.

He stood up, yawning, and advanced to the group lying as far as possible from the fire—for the night was stifling. He checked off the sleepers. Kenshaw—Ogden—Anderson—Ritters . . . Ellis? He caught himself glancing out to sea, and laughed nervously. Clark . . . but where was Clark? Landers went over the group again, but Clark was not among them.

"Clark!" Landers called softly. Then, when the call smote upon silence, "Clark!" he called more loudly. There was no answer. He raised his voice to a shout. The sleepers mumbled softly and sat up, one by one.

"What the devil!" grumbled Ogden. "Can't you wake him without gettin' the rest of us up?"

Landers' face in the firelight looked strained. Again he met Kenshaw's eye queerly. "He's not here. I can't make him hear me . . . Oh, Clark!" he bellowed loudly. But there was no reply.

"Do you suppose—" breathed Anderson, and stopped. But they knew what he had meant to say.

"I don't know," muttered the doctor. "Landers, light a stick of wood. We'll search the island . . . . "

They found him not far from the fire. His glassy eyes gleamed in the torchlight, and his throat was horrible to see.

"It got him, too!" breathed Ritters. "What if it—"

"Has anybody a gun?" asked Kenshaw quietly. Once more his eyes met Landers', but he glanced away quickly. "This simply means that whoever keeps watch will have to be armed . . . and keep close guard on the sleepers."

But no one had a gun. There was no weapon at all, it seemed, except the short pocket-knife they used to open oysters.

They buried Clark as they had done Ellis before him. The round of sentries had to be rearranged now, with those two missing. Ogden and the doctor were chosen after a short dispute, and another night was marked on Landers' log-calendar with a bit of shell.

Ogden huddled beside the fire, armed with the pocket-knife, eyes straining to pierce the darkness beyond the firelight. At every small stir made by the sleepers, he would start violently and glance this way and that in apprehension. Once he started to cry out, for he thought he saw something move among the sleeping forms a few yards away. But it was only one of his companions who had stood up and was moving slowly toward the fire. Ogden turned his head and stared again into the darkness out to sea, begrudging any moment he was not on the look-out for a passing ship. At that moment something tight and strong clutched this throat. The sentry tried to cry out, but only an inarticulate gurgle issued from his mouth. He was thrown violently to the cold sand . . . and then spinning lights and darkness fell upon him.

Kenshaw, rising at dawn, found him limp beside the dead fire, throat hideously mangled as Ellis's and Clark's had been. He woke the remaining three men, face very white, eyes wide with a fixed horror that seemed incongruous in a doctor—who knows all man can know of death.

"Landers," he spoke in a hushed whisper, "no sea-monster killed Ogden. Look! Look at those bruises on his neck!" He pointed a shaking finger at the thing on the sand, and expelled a shuddering sigh.

Landers met his eye sharply, and nodded.

"I noticed it before," he said quietly. "And you did, too. But I thought I must be mad—"

Kenshaw stared at the signal-flag unseeingly. "I should have told him. But . . . I thought . . . unless we were very sure . . . it was a horrible thing to say."

"What? What is it?" chattered the youth Anderson, glancing nervously from the doctor's face to Landers'. "What about the bruises?"

"Fingers," said Landers abruptly. "A man's fingers. And his throat," he brought out with a great effort, "—human teeth."

"Savages?" croaked Anderson, sickly green of face.

"We all know," Landers spoke tonelessly, "that there is no living thing on this island but ourselves." He paused and took a deep breath. *"It was one of us."*

Kenshaw gave a shuddering sigh and turned his eyes out toward the open sea. Anderson could only stare frozenly at the speaker. Ritters snorted.

"You're crazy," he said with vehemence. "One of us? Which one? Me, I guess." He laughed shortly. "I've knocked off many a guy," he told them grimly after a silence, "but not that way . . . ."

"No, no!" Anderson found his voice at last in a hysterical bleat. "No man could do that . . . it's . . . it's too horrible to think about."

"No man in his right mind, son," the doctor spoke gently. "But hunger—the insatiable longing for food, for meat—and monotony, and death staring him in the face, can do awful things to a man's reason. The ancients called it 'possession'—they'd say a demon entered one of our bodies and forced it to do things we could never in our senses do.

We would call it—I hardly know what. Cannibalism . . . homicidal manis, accompanied by lapse of memory. The seizure seems to come on after nightfall—it's a queer case—but whoever it is, doesn't remember anything about it when he . . . after it's over."

"But . . . it's hideous!" Anderson's eyes were dilated with horror. "It may be . . . *me.*" He began to sob suddenly like a terrified child. "What can we do? . . . what can we do?" he wailed.

"Steady, son." Kenshaw laid a gentle hand on the boy's shoulder. "Don't let it get you—don't think about it, or we'll . . . we'll all go mad," he jerked out. "We must just . . . watch each other . . . every minute."

There was no dispute as to sentry duty that night. No one thought of sleeping. They sat in a group about the fire, in strained silence, each cold with fear of what one of them might suddenly become—of what he himself might become. Ritters produced a pair of dice, forgotten since the wreck, and they gambled for pebbles in desperation for something to keep them from thinking.

It must have been about midnight that the ship passed. They saw its light, and began yelling wildly, piling more wood on the signal-fire, trying to beat out a code message with two stones. But the ship passed on without heeding them. They ran about the island frantically then, weeping and cursing . . . until Kenshaw's low cry brought them to their senses again. He was pointing to something that lay in the water at the island's far edge.

"Anderson!" he groaned. "Poor kid!" The remaining three men stared at each other woodenly. "Did anyone . . . watch me the whole time?" the doctor demanded.

Landers and Ritters shook their heads. In the frenzied excitement over the ship's passing, they had each forgotten the horror that hung over them like a dark cloud. And then suddenly Landers pointed to a dark spot on Ritters' soiled shirt-front. Kenshaw leaped forward and grasped the gunman by the arm. The small man turned deathly white.

"You . . . you mean . . . it was *me?*" choked Ritters. "How . . . how—"

Landers grasped his other arm and indicated the stained shirt in grim triumph. "Blood on your shirt, Ritters. It's the first trace that has been left . . . after . . . You got it there when you . . . Anderson," he mercifully left the words unsaid.

"Naw!" Ritters whispered desperately. "That ain't how I got it there! Look! I scratched my chest carrying wood to the fire . . . aw, hey, you can't think that I—"

"We can't take the chance, man," said Landers firmly. "We're going to tie you up until a ship comes." Ritters stared at them sickly. "Don't take it so—you didn't know. Couldn't help it. You're a sick man . . . . "

They trussed him hand and foot with their belts and bound him to a jutting bit of reef despite his pleas. And that night they slept without fear.

But morning brought a torrent of deeper horror than before rushing upon them. Ritters, bound and helpless as a baby, was the fifth victim. Like the rest he stared glassily at the sky, throat mangled as by the fangs of a wolf.

Landers met the doctor's frozen gaze grimly. "Well, Kenshaw," he spoke without inflection, "it's between us now."

Horror blazed in the doctor's eyes. "It's . . . unthinkable," he muttered. "One of us. You . . . *or me*." His lips twitched violently.

"Steady." Landers gripped his arm hard. "Don't let it get you, doc. There is still another possibility—someone else hidden on the island in some cave we haven't found." But both men knew that when the tide came in, any living creature that might be on the island must crouch with them on the small rise, or drown.

The day seemed winged, so much did they dread the coming of night. As the tide receded, they went about their task of gathering driftwood and digging for oysters. They talked incessantly, as though they feared the silence that swooped upon them when they ceased speaking. And as the sun sank below the horizon, the two survivors began to watch each other with increasing nervousness.

"I'll take this load of wood to the knoll," the doctor spoke with studied calm, squinting at the rim of sun above the sea-line. "Shall I open the oysters?" Landers nodded and handed him the pocket-knife.

What happened next was too quickly done for the eye to follow. With a quick snake-like gesture, Kenshaw slashed his left wrist well to the bone, transferred the blade, and slashed his right wrist in like manner. Landers sprang forward with a cry, but his companion smiled stonily and waved him back. Blood spurted from the gashes over the doctor's muscular hands—hands so skillful at the stanching of blood—and dripped upon the white sand where he stood.

"I couldn't stand it, old man—I'm sorry," he spoke quietly, and as Landers began to rip his soiled handkerchief into strips, "No, no! Don't try to stanch it—it wouldn't do any good. I've severed the artieries. It was the most painless way out."

Landers passed a shaking hand over his moist forehead. "How could you do a thing like that, Kenshaw?" he groaned. "There must be some other way out—"

Doctor Kenshaw shook his head gravely. "This is the only way, Landers. You see that, I know." He was breathing hard as blood pumped from the gashes at every beat of his heart. He sank to the sand weakly, a bitter little smile curving his lips. "I couldn't stand to know," he gasped. "And we'd have found out sooner or later . . . One of us . . . would know. And"—he sank upon his back, unable to support himself longer—"I couldn't take that knowledge into eternity with me, Landers. I'd rather die . . . not knowing . . . couldn't stand to know . . . I . . . was the . . . last man—" His voice trailed to a weak whisper, died away.

A familiar sound rose suddenly from the silence. Landers stood frozen with incredulity for a moment; then he whipped about and stared out to sea. In the dim twilight the clumsy form of a freighter was passing close to the island. Landers forgot the dying man, forgot everything in that instant of insane joy. He lit the signal-fire quickly and piled it high with wood that the scorching sun had dried. He waved his arms and screamed frantically, snatched up the flag and waved it aloft, waded waist-deep into the sea in foolish anxiety. But the ship had sighted their white flag, and already a boat was putting out from her toward the island.

Landers stumbled back to the doctor's side, sobbing with relief. He lifted the prone figure and shook Kenshaw violently, shouting the miracle over and over. But Doctor Kenshaw could not hear. The open knife was still clutched in his limp hand.

As the truth became apparent, a slow horror crept over Landers, chilling him to the soul. In that one madly joyous moment of seeing the rescue ship, he had forgotten something—something that swept over him now like an icy tide.

One of them—himself or the dead man at his feet—had hideously murdered five men, had torn out the throats of his five companions like a ravening beast. One of them—but which one? *Which one?*

Landers passed a trembling hand over his eyes. An impulse seized him to shout a warning to that approaching boat, to scream at them to go back and leave him there to die.

But suppose it was Kenshaw, lying now in a pool of his own blood shed in retribution for those five unthinkable crimes? Then he, Landers, had a right to go back and live among men. But . . . suppose it was *not* the doctor? Suppose he, Martin Landers, had sated his craving for meat by hideously slaughtering those five men? He thought of the coming night, on board the rescue freighter. He saw in imagination a stark figure—perhaps even one of those cheerfully waving men in the approaching boat—stretched out on a bloody deck, his throat mangled as by the teeth of a savage beast.

For there was no way he could be sure this madness would leave him—if, indeed, *he* was the man-monster—after he had left this accursed island. And home again, with an open door leading to little Marty's crib, to Helen's bed beside it . . . Landers groaned aloud. And even if those terrible seizures came upon him no more—*there were still Ellis . . . Clark . . . Ogden . . . Anderson . . . Ritters . . .*

Once more he glanced at the lifeless form at his feet. Yes, Kenshaw had taken the only way out. In any event, the doctor would have been killed or left with the mute evidence of a sixth mangled corpse—and either way, death was the only answer. If only he had stayed the knife-blow a few minutes longer, until the freighter blew her signal of rescue! But no—the fact would still have remained that one of them . . . one of them . . . yet if the madness returned, they would have caught the maniac on the ship, chained him like the wild thing he was, and the other man could have gone free. But now . . .

Landers stared dully at the oncoming boat. He could see the men's faces now, smiling encouragement, could hear their yells of reassurance. A bleak smile twisted his mouth.

"I'm the last man," he said aloud. "The last of seven." Cowardly of Kenshaw to leave him with that black question hanging over his head! It came to him clearly, like a sentence of death, that he could never know . . . unless at the cost of another poor devil's life. Landers bent slowly, loosened the pocket-knife from Kenshaw's limp fingers.

"Ahoy, mate!" shouted a man standing in the prow of the lifeboat. "We're a-comin'!"

Landers did not return the greeting. He tested the discolored blade in his hand with a calloused thumb. It was not very sharp—but sharp enough . . . .

Farnsworth Wright, the famous editor of WEIRD TALES, rarely named stories he felt were among the best he published. However, in response to a reader's query, he did name Mearle Prout's gruesome "The House of the Worm" as a story he felt had been unjustly ignored by most readers who named the best stories published in "the unique magazine." This story, one of only four that Prout had in WEIRD TALES, handles a familiar theme in a powerful manner. As Wright was prone to state, "An icy wind of horror blows through it."

MASQUERADE

Mearle Prout

"May I cut in, please?"

It was as simple as that. Yet, for all the gay masquerade throng, Donald shivered at the voice. He looked at the intruder and was not reassured. Tall and gaunt, the man was clad in the long flowing robes of a priest of ancient Egypt. His eyes were shaded, nearly covered by the black hood of his mask, but as he looked into them Donald had the uncanny impression of looking across a great dark void. Below the line of the mask the face was thin and creased, yellowed like old parchment.

With the barest trace of a smile the intruder bowed and said again, "If you don't mind."

Donald hesitated. Strangely, he felt his partner would not object if he were to refuse the very usual request. But to refuse would be unthinkable. He released his partner, and in a moment the tall man had whirled her away. Yet Donald was aware of her gaze upon him as he threaded across the crowded floor.

Away from the dancers, he paused and looked for the first time at the card she had slipped into his hand.

"Leonora Starr."

The name was printed in simple pica type; beyond that, the card was blank.

He frowned at first, then smiled. She so obviously expected him to see her again. He recalled with pleasure her lithe surrender to his arms while they danced, the warmth with which she had pressed the small card into his hand.

Who was she? he wondered. The name, Leonora Starr, told him nothing. They had met less than five minutes before, and even then had spoken but little.

The music of the waltz rose to a higher, more exciting strain. Donald searched the crowd with his eyes until he found her, still dancing with the mysterious stranger. They were at the south end of the ballroom now, near the door that led into the garden. The tall man, Donald noted, danced gracefully but stiffly, as though he had once been an excellent dancer, but was now long out of practice.

Across the crowd Donald caught Leonora's eye, and something flashed between them. An appeal, he thought it was. His pulse raced while he stared across the intervening space, and then—his glance clashed with that of the giant. He was conscious of the same chilling sensation at the pit of his stomach, as though he were falling; felt the same prickling at the roots of his hair. . . . Then, in another whirl of the dance, the man had turned away.

A little group of people near by was not dancing. Donald strolled toward them, halted half-way and looked back across the floor. He felt a light touch at his elbow.

"That man who tagged you—who is he?" said Betty Cosgrove as he turned. She was obviously agitated.

"I've been wondering. Doesn't anyone know?"

"No—except that he wasn't invited."

"Are—you sure? It might be just the costume."

"No—none of the guests is so tall. Besides, he wasn't announced." She shuddered.

"He—he looks like a death's-head, or a mummy. If he asks me to dance, I'll faint."

Abruptly the music ceased, to be replaced by the hum of voices and scattered applause. Apprehensive now in spite of himself, Donald shouldered his way through the crowd in search of Leonora. She was not on the floor. Hurriedly he surveyed the guests again. The man too had disappeared. The garden, perhaps?

Quickly he stepped to the door. There was no moon, but the garden was dimly lighted by a single Japanese lantern hung near the center. Donald could see no one. Dense shrubbery bordered the walks, and in the far corner a thick grove of trees loomed black in the shadows. He drew a deep breath and walked swiftly toward it.

Behind him the music began again, a haunting Viennese melody in waltz time. He looked back at the lighted windows. People, in their brilliant costumes, were again taking the floor. No one else had come out after him; to all appearances he was alone in the garden. He hesitated, half minded to turn back. Fool's errand!

Suddenly, above the music, he heard a woman scream, a muffled scream that was not repeated. It came from the grove of trees. His heart leaping, he turned and ran toward it, searching his pockets for a weapon as he ran. There was none.

He reached the trees. It was not as dark there as it had seemed. The level rays of the Japanese lantern, though dim, shone redly through the shadows. Suddenly in his haste he stumbled over a creeper of vine, and, catching himself, stopped short at the sight before him.

At this spot the heavy growth of trees gave way to a circular clearing, and the ground was covered by a lush carpet of grass. The light of the Japanese lantern seemed to filter undiminished through the trees and become amplified at this spot, so that everything which occurred was as clear to the watcher as in the light of day. And at the very center of the circle, at the top of a small rise, was the horrifying tableau. Leonora was lying on her side, her face half buried in the grass; over her, his knee on her shoulder, his left hand covering her mouth, was the tall man in the priestly robe. In his right hand he held aloft a glittering knife with a long curved blade, which he held poised in a perpetual threat. He had not yet struck.

The man, disheveled by the struggle, could be seen better now. From the arm which held the knife aloft the robe had fallen away, revealing it to the shoulder; it was thin as bone, it had the appearance of bone stretched tightly over with yellow, parchment-like skin. His headdress was lost, revealing a smooth hairless head which seemed deathly white even in the red rays of the lantern. The mask, too, was gone, and his eyes—in the shadows they appeared like something which Donald, if he were to remain sane, dared not think about.

A cold perspiration beading his skin, Donald looked about him for a weapon, while the two before him held the same motionless pose. A stone, a broken limb of a tree, any weapon would suffice—if only the demon did not strike, if only Leonora could hold him bck a moment longer! In his excitement he never wondered why he had not already done so, why, if he wished to kill, he had not killed and fled minutes before. Nor did he wonder how Leonora, facing death, could wait for it so passively. If he had stopped to think of those things, to realize their meaning, perhaps he might have noticed other, more obvious, circumstances: that the music, which had sounded so loudly in the garden a few seconds before, had died to nothing the moment he had entered the hellish grove; that the light breeze from out of the west no longer fanned his cheek, and now did not even rustle the leaves of the trees; that the very starlight seemed to drip unwillingly through the interlaced branches overhead . . . .

Twenty feet to the left, Donald saw a spade leaning against a tree. He started for it, but at that moment a sudden burst of activity on the part of Leonora freed her mouth and she called weakly,

"Quickly—help!"

Being young, Donald could not resist that appeal. He left the spade untouched, and turned and ran to fling himself against the gaunt attacker.

With a single bound the other rose to meet his attack, the knife drawn to strike, the lips snarling. The girl too rose to her feet and stood.

"Back to the house, Leonora—run!" shouted Donald. He had halted, crouched ready to spring, ten feet from the towering skeleton before him.

But the girl stood still, apparently tense with excitement.

"You must kill him," she hissed, "or he'll kill me."

"Who is he?" Donald rasped.

"He's—a priest," she lied. "His name is Ozaman."

Donald knew that she was lying, though he could not tell how he knew it—nor why she was.

"Go to the house," he said again, "and send some men out; I'll keep him here."

A sardonic smile twisted the features of Ozaman.

"You—don't want me alone?" he taunted.

In that instant it happened. Leonora had crept up behind the priest; suddenly she charged him, grasped the hand that held the knife. The priest swung upon her, ready to crash a heavy fist upon her face. Donald rushed in.

He caught the blow in the chest. It staggered him. Then with all his power he flung himself forward and closed.

Donald was athletic. In college he had been a member of the wrestling team, had been rated fair at boxing. But he knew in a second that he had underrated his opponent. The arms of this fleshless skeleton were like bands of steel, the legs as firm as if rooted in the ground. Suddenly Ozaman laughed. He tossed the knife from him, picked Donald up bodily, whirled him through the air until he was dizzy, then threw him to the ground with stunning force. Then he dropped quickly upon him and pinned his arms to the ground.

Donald lay on his back in the grass, helpless. staring up at the twin caverns of the monster's eyes. A wave of revulsion shook him, left him weak and pale, his body wet with sweat. Those eyes again! Was he insane? But he knew that he was not. This was real. This was happening! Back there, behind those trees, was the ballroom, and a gay throng, and music, and laughter. And here—this!

His mind, stimulated by terror, worked fast. The knife! It had been lost in the struggle. Then, surely, Leonora—she twisted his head to look for her. She was standing on his left ten feet away, her eyes shining, her lips slightly parted.

He called to her. "Find the knife—and hurry!" he said.

She made no reply, but stood smiling, neutral. A gleam in the grass near her caught his eye.

"What's the matter? It's there at your feet. Help me!" he shouted.

As she made no move he realized that she would not—that what was to be done he must do for himself. A black rage gave new strength to his arms. She must be in league with the priest! She had confessed to knowing him . . . . He saw now that he had been lured into this unequal contest. But why?

The priest tightened his hold on Donald's arms again, so that Donald writhed with the pain.

"Why are you holding me? What do you want? he cried at last.

"Only your body," said Ozaman softly.

His body! The man was insane?

If only he could reach the knife—if he could get an arm free!

He feigned a struggle, edging toward the knife as he fought. When he was again overcome, he was two feet nearer. He rested. Then another struggle, another two feet gained. He had a feeling the priest was playing with him as a cat plays with a mouse, encouraging him to escape and then dashing his hopes. Well, there might be a surprise! . . . .

Two more pretended struggles, and the knife was within his reach. Now if an arm were free . . . .

Suddenly the priest bent his head low, so that his fetid breath seared the nostrils of the prostrate man.

"I'm going to kill you now," he said.

Simultaneously he loosed Donald's arms and clutched his neck with bony fingers. Donald felt the breath in his lungs pent up, fighting for escape while he flailed his left arm in search of the knife. He grasped the smooth handle, balanced it a moment in his hand. He focused his staring eyes upon the figure leaning low over him, aimed his blow well. As he struck, the priest inclined his head to the left, leaving a clean path for the knife. It severed the veins in his neck.

At once Donald felt his body galvanized as from an electric shock. He was aware of a mighty force penetrating his brain. Red flashes seemed to shoot from the priest's eyes, to play into his own. Giddiness and nausea as in a violent earthquake racked his consciousness. And then, for a moment, he fainted away.

When he again opened his eyes the scene was, to all appearances, unchanged. Over him were the same trees, the same . . . He raised his hand to a gutting pain in his throat, felt something warm spurt over it. He looked. Blood! But surely this was not his own hand—this was thin, and bony. The garment which covered the arm was not his own either, but white and flowing—the garment of a priest! The words of Ozaman resounded in his brain like a death-knell:

"I want your body!"

And now his dimming eyes beheld a scene which tore his soul with despair. A man, clad as he had been, with the same proud tilt of the head, the same athletic carriage, but with eyes which glittered strangely now in the pale light, stepped toward a beautiful girl.

"Come, Leonora," he said, in a voice which Donald recognized as his own. "It is time to go."

She looked at him with a slow smile.

"You really are very, very handsome, Ozaman," she answered.

And as the eyes of the prostrate figure slowly filmed in death the now perfectly matched pair looked back at him and laughed with wild abandon.

On checking previous appearances of the stories in this collection, "Naked Lady" turned out to be the most anthologized. It has appeared twice before, once in hardcover in 1940 and then in a rare paperback in 1946. So the chances are that it will be unfamiliar to the average reader and the story is just too good not to be included in this collection. Mindret Lord wrote for several of the horror and weird fiction pulps of the thirties. The unique idea in this tale makes it by far her best work.

NAKED LADY

Mindret Lord

Marion Van Orton finished packing her dressing-case, opened her purse to make sure that her steamer tickets were still there, took one last look in the mirror and then descended the wide, polished staircase of the Van Orton mansion for the last time. Gorham, the butler, met her at the door.

"Madam will be gone for the weekend?" he asked.

"Including the weekend," Mrs. Van Orton amended.

The town car was waiting at the curb. He helped her into it and stood waiting at the door while she settled back comfortably. She looked up questioningly.

"Will Madam leave any message?" Gorham asked.

"Oh," she sighed, "just say I've gone."

"For an indefinite stay, Madam?"

Languidly, Mrs. Van Orton motioned to the chauffeur. "No," she said. "Just say I've gone."

The purring motor drew away. Only Gorham's eyes moved as he watched it turn the corner. With a start he recovered himself and closed his mouth. "Well!" he said as he walked up the stairs. A greater degree of volubility had returned to him when he reported the incident to the cook.

Just for the moment, Gilda Ransome's life had crystallized into one desperate wish: if she couldn't scratch her thigh, this instant, she would go stark, raving mad. A few hours earlier she had thought that if she didn't have breakfast life would be insupportable. Hunger was bad enough—but this itch!

"You may rest now," said Mr. Blake, the well-known designer of the fleshier covers of the naughtier magazines. He turned away and lit a cigarette. Gilda applied her nails to her skin as she went behind a screen and drew on a dressing-gown.

82

She began to think about her hunger again. She was not hungry because she was on a reducing diet—she needed neither reduction nor addition. Every artist for whom she had posed had agreed that her figure was "just the type"—presumably the type that sells magazines. And her face was certainly no less attractive than her figure—which is an emphatic statement.

She felt starved because influenza had kept her idle for three weeks and during that time her money had run out. She had never been one to save.

Later in the day she fainted while trying to hold a tiring pose. Mr. Blake was very much annoyed, and he determined that in the future he would use stronger, if less perfect, models.

In the West Indies there were many, many men who would have testified to the cleverness of Jeremiah Van Orton. As a lad of twenty he had come to Curacao from Holland, and for forty-five years thereafter he had remained in the Indies. Then he had decided that he was too rich and too old to go on working. That was his first mistake. If he had kept his nose to the grindstone, he would not have come to New York. He would not have met Marion Martin, the actress. He would not have made a fool of himself.

Van Orton sat huddled in front of an open fire and thought the matter over. In this climactic hour he paused to review his life and works.

Vivid flashes of memory confused his efforts to keep his thoughts orderly. A tongue of flame licked around a log in the fireplace. A thread of scented smoke curled into the room . . . . A night in the Haitian jungle—when was it? Twenty—thirty years ago? A black wench was dying. "For no reason," the doctor said; "for superstition. Voodoo." . . . Marion Martin had been convincing. She had said that she was tired of young men—men whom she could not respect. She had said a man was not in his prime until sixty or seventy. Until then, he was callow, unproved, not worthy of admiration or love. He knew nothing of metropolitan people. He had been attracted to her and, presently, he had believed and loved her . . . What was that about the natives destroying with such care every fingernail cutting, every hair? One had to be careful—voodoo was strong in the West Indies . . . He had given Marion his honorable name and a million dollars besides. Even if she hadn't pretended to love him, he might have done the same. She had given him the illusion of youth. He had thought of a future with her, for her. He might have lived forever!

And now he was nothing but an old fool who was going to die. But so was she. Oh, yes, so was she!

The idea of following his wife to wherever she might come to rest and murdering her there never occurred to Jeremiah Van Orton. He was too tired and feeble for such a melodramatic role. One did not spend a lifetime in the Indies for nothing. He was clever; except for this little interlude of marriage, he had always been clever. He would find a way, a good way—a safe way for him, an unpleasant way for her.

Jeremiah Van Orton could always think better among his beautiful collection of paintings. He went to the drawing-room and drew up a chair before a Hobbema landscape. There he remained until he had planned all the details of his vengeance.

In the restaurant of the Hotel Lafayette, Michael Bonze sat across the table from his friend, Pierre Vanneau, and cursed the age in which they both were born.

"What does art mean in the Twentieth Century?" he asked rhetorically. "Nothing! People talk about the dynamic beauty of a new streamlined toilet seat or the Empire State Building. Or take Surrealism: daubs —damn it!—daubs by clumsy, color-blind house-painters! Picasso eats while I starve! Cocteau is the white-haired boy while I worry myself bald! People don't want things to look like what they are—they want them to look like the sublimation of the mood of the essence of the psychological reaction to what they might be if they weren't what they are. Oh, I know it sounds like sour grapes, but I wouldn't mind if it weren't for the fact that I'm a painter with greater talent than any of them. If I were living in Henry the Eighth's time, people would now be collecting Bonzes instead of Holbeins. Damn the Twentieth Century!"

"Look," said Vanneau, "have you ever painted a beautiful young girl? You know—curves and flowing hair and so on?"

Bonze slapped his big hand down on the table top and the dishes jumped. "Are you trying to be insulting?" he bellowed. "Do you take me for Henry Clive?—or—or Zuloaga, maybe? No! No, I haven't painted any pretty valentines of beautiful young girls!"

Vanneau murmured into his coffee cup, "Rubens did. Tiepolo did. Titian did . . . ."

"Oh, shut up!" said Bonze. "You know what I meant. People won't take that sort of thing from a modern artist—it isn't art. Art is old, wrinkled-up men, or nauseous arrangements of dried fish and rotten apples, or anything sufficiently ugly and nasty."

"How do you know that is so?" Vanneau asked. "What modern artist has dared to paint a *pretty* picture? I don't know of anyone since Greuze, and his picture sold well enough."

"Well—" Bonze began doubtfully.

"And look," Vanneau continued, "in this jaded age, sex appeal is important. Important? It is everything!" He spread out his arms in an all-embracing gesture. "And what do you create for an avid public? A public that waters at the mouth at the very mention of nudism or Mae West? You give them old men and dried fish! Don't weep on *my* shoulder—you give me a pain!"

Bronze was still feeling a little sorry for himself. "I give Meyergold, the critic, a pain, too. Today, he came to the studio and said he didn't think I was ready, just yet, to have a show. He stayed about fifteen minutes. Damn him!"

On the morning following his wife's departure, Jeremiah Van Orton engaged the services of a Mr. Moses Winkler, a student of biology, who was promised double payment if he could manage to get through his work without asking questions. He was led into a lady's boudoir and told that he must go over the entire room with a microscope in order to collect every human remain, no matter how small or apparently unimportant.

Mr. Van Orton watched every move he made. Somehow, Moses did not like the eagerness with which the old man greeted each new find. It made him quite nervous.

When Moses finished his work he was able to deliver to his employer a surprising number of small envelopes, on each of which he had written a description of the contents. One held grains of dust from a nail-file; another, an eyelash. On a brush in the bathroom he had found a few flakes of skin. A minute drop of blood had been discovered on a hand-kerchief in the laundry basket . . . . The list went on.

Moses was paid and dismissed. He was glad to go.

Van Orton added the envelopes to a collection he had made of all the photographs of his wife that she had left in the house. He looked long at the relics before locking them safely away.

"It is not a great deal," he muttered to himself, "but in Haiti I've known them to do it with less—much less."

Within a month, old Mr. Van Orton had become the scandal of Sutton Place. Every day, from nine until six, a constant stream of handsome young women entered and left his house. Much to Gorham's bewilderment and disapproval, it had become his master's custom to sit in the drawing-room and interview the young ladies, one by one. Discreet inquiries elicited the fact that they were artists' models answering a newspaper advertisement.

"What," Gorham had asked the cook, "does the old reprobate want with a model? And if he wants a model, why is he so hard to satisfy? He must have seen two hundred of them already and he's not kept one over ten minutes.''

It was the cook's considered opinion that Jeremiah Van Orton was an indecent, dirty old man who should be put away where he couldn't do any harm.

The procession of applicants ended when Gilda Ransome was ushered into the drawing-room. Gorham was called and told that no more models would be seen. He breathed a sigh of relief and stole a glance at the young lady who had been chosen from among so many. Gorham had a shock—for a second he had thought she was Mrs. Van Orton. It was a startling resemblance.

Michael Bonze sat in his studio window and looked at the dreary square with bare trees and muddy streets. It was a picture of his mood. His money was running low and he was thinking that he ought to be putting in a stock of canned baked beans instead of buying a half-case of gin. There was nothing he wanted to paint. He hated painting and art patrons and critics.

A sedate foreign limousine came splashing along the street below and stopped at the door to his studio building. The sight didn't make him any happier. "Art patron!" he said with a wealth of expression in his voice.

In a moment there was a knock on the door, and Michael opened it to admit Jeremeah Van Orton.

"You are Michael Bonze?'' he asked.

Bonze admitted his identity, although, just then, he was not particularly proud of it. The caller presented his card with the question, "You have heard of me?''

"Yes,'' said Bonze; "I've heard you have quite a large collection of Flemish paintings. Will you take a chair?''

Van Orton launched into his business at once. "I have come to see you,'' he said, "because I want a special kind of painting which you do better than anyone I know.''

"Thank you!'' Michael murmured and crossed his fingers behind him.

"Not that I like the sort of painting you do,'' the old man continued, "on the contrary, I dislike it intensely. It is dull, spiritless— I might say, insipid.''

"Oh, do say 'insipid'!'' said Michael. "Also say 'goodbye,' sir, at once!''

"Come, come!'' said Van Orton, calmly. "This is no time for compliments. I am not here to discuss art but to make you a proposition which you will find highly beneficial, financially.''

Bonze had a sudden vision of rows of canned baked beans, and he held his tongue.

''For a particular reason, which is none of your affair, I wish you to paint a lifesize nude of a model I have selected. The pose makes very little difference, but I suggest that you have her reclining on a chaise-lounge. For background you may use drapery or anything you please— it is of no importance.''

Bonze asked, ''Would you mind telling me why I should have been chosen for this work?''

''Because your painting is so realistically accurate that not even a colored photograph can compare with it. I don't consider it art, but it will serve my purpose.''

After all, a man had to have some pride. ''I'm not interested,'' said Bonze.

No shade of disappointment crossed the old man's face. ''No, no,'' he agreed, ''of course not. But you would, perhaps, be interested in fifteen thousand dollars, a third payable now?''

Michael resisted an impulse to jump up and kiss the beneficent bald head. ''Write the check and send me the model,'' he said. ''I'll start today.''

''Good!'' said Van Orton. ''But now I must lay down two important conditions. First, I will give you a number of photographs of a young woman who bears some resemblance to the model you will use. I want you to study the pictures very closely, because your painting must look more like them than like the model.''

''But why,'' Michael protested, ''why can't I simply paint a portrait of the subject of the photographs? It would be a lot more satisfactory and easier.''

''If the job were as easy as that, I wouldn't be paying you fifteen thousand dollars.'' Van Orton reached in the pocket of his coat and withdrew ten or twelve little envelopes. ''The second request that I must make is this,'' He continued. ''Each of these packets contains a pinch of powder. They are plainly marked, 'hair, nails, skin, lips,' and so on. Now when you mix your paints for these various details, you must add these powders as indicated. You are a man of honor?''

''Certainly!'' said the very mystified painter.

''You will give me your word that this will be done according to my instructions?''

Michael nodded.

''Very well. Here is my check for five thousand dollars. Hurry your work as much as you can with safety and let me know the instant it is done.'' Van Orton went to the door. ''I brought the model with me in the car. I will send her up with the photographs. Good day!''

Bonze collapsed into a chair as the door closed.

Spring has come to Venice and the Piazza San Marco has a freshly washed and burnished look. Mrs. Van Orton sits at Florian's on the edge of the square, sipping a Pernod. She feels that God's in His Heaven and Life is Just a Bowl of Cherries.

Mrs. Van Orton has a figure that looks well in anything, but its effectiveness increases in inverse ratio with the amount of clothing she wears; hence, to some extent, Venice and the Lido. When she walks along the beach, this summer, the women will turn away and the men will turn toward her. The women will say, ''Who is that doll-faced American in the daring bathing-costume?'' The men are discreet on the Lido—they will say nothing. But they will look.

And spring has come to Washington Square. The old trees are beginning to think about their Easter clothing. Probably they will decide that the well-dressed tree will wear a very light and delicate chartreuse. Feathers, too, may be worn.

Michael Bonze looked up from his painting. ''Darling,'' he said, ''you're the best work I've ever done. And you're just about finished.''

''Thank goodness!'' said Gilda Ransome. ''May I move, now?''

''Go ahead,'' he said. ''Get up and we'll make some coffee.''

He put down his palette and brushes and helped her into her kimono, kissing, as he did so, the back of her neck.

''I wonder,'' he said, ''if I could have done such a good portrait if I hadn't fallen in love with you. I owe a lot to old Van Orton. If it hadn't been for him—and tor Pierre Vanneau—''

''Why Pierre Vanneau?'' she asked.

Michael smiled in memory of his annoyance. ''It was he who first suggested that I paint beautiful women. I was furious.''

''So shall I be,'' said Gilda, ''if you dare to paint any woman but me.''

''Never fear!'' he laughed. ''There will be no one but you. I'll paint you as everything from Medusa to the Virgin Mary.''

''I *might* make a Medusa,'' said Gilda.

Later in the day, the picture was finished to the immense satisfaction of both artist and model.

The next morning Michael arose before Gilda was awake. He wanted to look at the portrait in the cold light of dawn. Without, he told himself, undue self-praise, he found it good—very good. Maybe it wasn't modern, maybe the style wasn't original, perhaps it wasn't spontaneous. But the draftsmanship, the color, the texture, the composition—that was all perfect. No one could deny it. It would take no violent stretch of the imagination to conceive the beautiful creature rising from her couch and stepping lightly down from the canvas to the floor.

Bonze thought it wasn't fair that this, his best work, was destined to be hung in a dark, lonely house, among a lot of gloomy Flemish paintings, for the exclusive pleasure of a solitary old Dutchman. After all, Art was for the masses. If Meyergold could see this, he'd sing a different tune. If if weren't for the money, he'd never let Van Orton have the picture—the insulting old idiot! He wouldn't appreciate it, anyway. It wouldn't have made any difference to him if the picture had been good or bad. All he wanted was a likeness.

On the heels of this reflection, Bonze realized in a flash of inspiration how he could keep his picture. He would make a copy and give *that* to Van Orton. Naturally, it wouldn't be so good as the original, but what of that? He hadn't promised to deliver a masterpiece. Of course, there was the matter of those little packets of powder—he'd used it all in the original—but—well, it was silly, anyway.

He woke Gilda with a shout and told her his plan. "I'll have the thing finished by the end of the week. Then I'll get my check and we'll go right down to the City Hall and be married."

Gilda looked at the clock on the bed table. "Is this a nice hour to propose to a girl?" she groaned and pulled the covers over her head.

Whistling loudly and cheerfully, Michael started to work.

Jeremiah Van Orton crouched before the likeness of his wife lying nude upon a chaise-lounge. He had never seen her so. She had always kept him at arm's length. But now she was near—near enough to touch with the finger tips, or a long pin, or a keen-edged knife.

Though never for a moment did he take his mad gaze from the portrait, he did not neglect the task at which he worked. Methodically, he sharpened on a whetstone a number of efficient-looking probes and knives. The scrape of the steel and his panting breath were the only sounds in the darkened room. Incessantly, he moistened his opened lips with his tongue. His heart pounded in his ears.

Jeremiah knew that the excitement of the execution was killing him, that he must hurry. He got to his feet and addressed the painting in a high, cracked voice.

"Marion," he said, "I hold your life in this image by virtue of your skin and blood. Do you understand? This is you!"

He tried the point of a blue steel probe against this thumb. His voice rose to a shriek.

"You are going to die, Marion, my love, wherever you are!"

His bloodshot eyes fixed themselves in a hypnotic stare as he approached the portrait. Great veins throbbed in his shriveled neck and temples.

"Excellent!" said Mr. Meyergold. "Really excellent! I must say, my dear Bonze, you surprise me!"

He looked around with an expression frequently worn by owners of dogs that are able to sit up or shake hands. He assumed an air of patronizing pride. He reasoned that he had played an important part in the development of this young artist by his stern and uncompromising rejection, until now, of everything he had done. He turned again to the picture and nodded. Bonze was a good dog and it was no more than fair to throw him a bone—he had earned it. "Excellent!" he repeated. "What do you call it?"

"I call it," said Michael, racking his brain for a likely name, "I call it 'Naked Lady'."

Mr. Meyergold glanced up sharply. "Naked Lady." He rolled it around on this tongue. "Good! Oh, very good! A fine distinction. This is no ordinary nude; no allegorical Grecian goddess to whom a yard of drapery more or less makes no difference." He thought that an awfully good line for a review and decided to make a note of it the instant he left. He laughed in appreciation of his wit. "Oh, no, this young lady is shy and embarrassed without her clothing." He went on enlarging the idea in the hope that he would hit upon another useful line. "Here you've caught a lady in a most undignified situation. I get the impression that your 'Naked Lady' is very much annoyed with us for looking at her."

In her cabin on the beach, Marion Van Orton was changing from her bathing-suit to an elaborate pair of pajamas. Suddenly she had a distinct impression that she was being observed. She jerked a bath-towel up to her chest and swung around. Apparently there was nothing to account for her fear. But she *knew* that someone was minutely examining her. Hurriedly, she pulled on her pajamas and ran from the cabin, fully expecting to surprise some rude man in the act of staring through a chink in the wall. There was no one near.

In spite of the heat of the day, she went back into the cabin and wrapped a heavy cloak tightly about her. Still the miserable feeling persisted.

"My goodness!" she said to herself, "I feel positively naked!"

A month later, Marion Van Orton had cause to remember that day on the Lido. She was sitting in the Excelsior Bar, reading a *New York Times*, two weeks old. She had really been looking through it to see if there were any more news of the death of her husband. For a few days the papers had been full of "Millionaire Husband of Actress Found Dead." When she had first heard of it she had wondered which of the paintings it was that had been found slashed to rags and tatters, and she wondered what had happened before his heart failed that had made him want to ruin one of the pictures of which he had always been so proud.

There was nothing more in the *Times*. The story had been squeezed dry and dropped in favor of an expedition to the South Pole. Finishing a rather dull announcement of the forthcoming exhibit of paintings by an artist who had just married his model, Marion turned to her handsome companion.

"Some people insist," she said, "that more important things happen in New York than here, or anywhere else. But look at this paper; there isn't an interesting or important thing in it. It's all too, too boring for words."

And then, quite suddenly, that awful nightmarish feeling returned to her. She was entirely naked and people were looking at her, criticizing her, appraising her. As she crossed her arms at her throat, her eyes darted about the room, searching for the guilty Peeping Tom. She could detect no one, but she knew, she *knew* that to someone her clothing was perfectly transparent.

Without excusing herself to her startled friend, Mrs. Van Orton jumped up and rushed to her room in the hotel. She locked and bolted the door. The sensation was growing stronger every moment. She pulled down the shades and turned off the light. But it was no better. She ran into the clothes closet and shut the door. Even there, there was no escape from the certain knowledge that she was bare and defenseless before a crowd. She drew the hanging dresses tightly around her and shrank into a corner of the closet. She felt she was going mad.

This story is one of those found in a large box of papers belonging to Robert E. Howard found by Glenn Lord, the executor of the Howard estate, a few years ago. It was published in THE MAGAZINE OF HORROR but has never appeared in any hardcover or paperback collection. It is a typical Howard story of horror and heroism, independent of any of his series adventures.

OUT OF THE DEEP

Robert E. Howard

Adam Falcon sailed at dawn, and Margaret Deveral, the girl who was to marry him, stood on the wharfs in the cold mist to wave a good-bye. At the dusk Margaret knelt, stony-eyed, above the still white form that the crawling tide had left crumpled on the beach.

The people of Faring town gathered about, whispering. "The fog hung heavy; mayhap she went ashore on Ghost Reef. Strange that his corpse alone should drift back to Faring harbor—and so swiftly."

And an undertone. "Alive or dead, he would come to her!"

The body lay above the tide mark, as if flung by a vagrant wave; slim, but strong and virile in life, now darkly handsome even in death. The eyes were closed, strange to say, so it appeared that he but slept. The seaman's clothes he wore had fragments of seaweed clinging to them.

"Strange," muttered old John Harper, owner of the Sea-lion Inn, and the oldest ex-seaman of Faring town. "He sank deep, for these weeds grow only at the bottom of the ocean, aye, in the coral-grown caves of the sea."

Margaret spoke no word, she but knelt, her hands pressed to her cheeks, eyes wide and staring.

"Take him in your arms, lass, and kiss him," gently urged the people of Faring, "for 'tis what he would have wished, alive."

The girl obeyed mechanically, shuddering at the coldness of the body. Then as her lips touched his, she screamed and recoiled.

"This is not Adam!" she shrieked, staring wildly about her.

The people nodded sadly to each other.

"Her brain is turned," the whispered, and then they lifted the corpse and bore it to the house wherein Adam Falcon had lived—where he had hoped to bring his bride when he returned from his voyage.

And the people brought Margaret along with them, caressing her and soothing her with gentle words. But the girl walked like one in a trance, her eyes still staring in that strange manner.

They laid the body of Adam Falcon on his bed, with death candles at the head and feet, and the salt water from his garments trickled off the bed and splashed on the floor. For it is a superstition in Faring town, as on many dim coasts, that monstrously bad luck will follow if a drowned man's clothes are removed.

And Margaret sat there in the death room and spoke to none, staring fixedly at Adam's dark calm face. And, as she sat, John Gower, a rejected suitor of hers, and a moody, dangerous man, came and, looking over her shoulder, said; "Sea death brings a curious change, if that is the Adam Falcon I knew."

Black looks were passed his way, whereat he seemed surprised; and men rose and quietly escorted him to the door.

"You hated Adam Falcon, John Gower," said Tom Leary, "and you hate Margaret because the child preferred a better man than you. Now, by Satan, you'll not be torturing the girl with your calloused talk. Get out and stay!"

Gower scowled darkly at this, but Tom Leary stood up boldly to him, and the men of Faring town back of him, so John turned his back squarely upon them and strode away. Yet to me it had seemed that what he had said had not been meant as a taunt or an insult, but simply the result of a sudden, startling thought.

And as he walked away I heard him mutter to himself;" . . . Alike, and yet strangely unlike him . . . " Night had fallen on Faring town and the windows of the houses blinked through the darkness; through the windows of Adam Falcon's house glimmered the death candles where Margaret and others kept silent watch until dawn. And beyond the friendly warmth of the town's lights, the dusky green titan brooded along the strand, silent now as if in sleep, but ever ready to leap with hungry talons. I wandered down to the beach and, reclining on the white sand, gazed out over the slowly heaving expanse which coiled and billowed in drowsy undulations like a sleeping serpent.

The sea—the great, gray, cold-eyed woman of the ages. Her tides spoke to me as they have spoken to me since birth—in the swish of the flat waves along the sand, in the wail of the ocean-bird, in her throbbing silence. *I am very old and very wise* (brooded the sea), *I have no part of man; I slay men and even their bodies I fling back upon the cowering land. There is life in my bosom, but it is not human life* (whispered the sea), *my children hate the sons of men.*

A shriek shattered the stillness and brought me to my feet, gazing wildly about me. Above the stars gleamed coldly, and their scintillant ghosts sparkled on the ocean's cold surface. The town lay dark and still, save for the death lights in Adam Falcon's house—and the echoes still shuddering through the pulsating silence.

I was among the first to arrive at the door of the death room and there halted aghast with the rest. Margaret Deveral lay dead upon the floor, her slender form crushed like a slim ship among shoals, and crouching over her, cradling her in his arms, was John Gower, the gleam of insanity in his wide eyes. And the death candles still flickered and leaped, but no corpse lay on Adam Falcon's bed.

"God's mercy!" gasped Tom Leary. "John Gower, ye fiend from hell, what devil's work is this?"

Gower looked up.

"I told you," he shrieked. "She knew—and I knew—'twas not Adam Falcon, that cold monster flung up by the mocking waves! 'Tis some demon inhabiting his corpse! Hark—I sought my bed and tried to sleep, but each time there came the thought of this soft girl sitting beside that cold inhuman thing you thought her lover, and at last I rose and came to the window. Margaret sat, drowsing, and the others, fools that they were, slept in other parts of the house. And as I watched . . ."

He shook as a wave of shuddering passed over him.

"As I watched, Adam's eyes opened, and the corpse rose swift stealthy from the bed where it lay. I stood without the window frozen, helpless, and the ghastly thing stole upon the unknowing girl, with frightful eyes burning with hellish light and snaky arms outstretched. Then, she woke and screamed and then—oh Mother of God!— the dead man lapped her in his terrible arms, and she died without a sound."

Gower's voice died out into incoherent gibberings, and he rocked the dead girl gently to and fro like a mother with a child.

Tom Leary shook him. "Where is the corpse?"

"He fled into the night," said John Gower tonelessly.

Men looked at each other, bewildered.

"He lies," muttered they, deep in their beards. "He has slain Margaret himself and hidden the corpse somewhere to bear out his ghastly tale."

A sullen snarl shook the throng, and as one man they turned and looked where, on Hangman's Hill overlooking the bay, Lie-lip Canool's bleached skeleton glimmered against the stars.

They took the dead girl from Gower's arms, though he clung to her, and laid her gently on the bed between the candles meant for Adam Falcon. Still she lay, and white, and men and women whispered that she seemed more like one drowned than one crushed to death.

We bore John Gower through the village streets, he not resisting; but seeming to walk in a daze muttering to himself. But in the square, Tom Leary halted.

"This is a strange tale Gower told us," said he, "and doubtless a lie. Still, I am not a man to be hanging another without certainty. Therefore, let us place him in the stocks for safekeeping, while we search for Adam's corpse. Time enough for hanging afterwards."

So this was done and as we turned away, I looked back upon John Gower, who sat, head bowed upon his breast, like a man who is weary unto death.

So, under the dim wharfs and in the attics of houses and among stranded hulls we searched for Adam Falcon's corpse. Back up into the hills behind the town our hunt lead us, where we broke up into groups and couples and scattered out over the barren downs.

My companion was Michael Hansen, and we had gotten so far apart that the darkness cloaked him from me, when he gave a sudden shout. I started toward him, and then the shout broke into a shriek and the shriek died off into grisly silence. Michael Hansen lay dead on the earth, and a dim form slunk away in the gloom as I stood above the corpse, my flesh crawling.

Tom Leary and the rest came on the run and gathered about, swearing that John Gower had done this deed, also.

"He has escaped, somehow, from the stocks," said they, and we legged it for the village at top speed.

Aye, John Gower had escaped from the stocks and from his townsmen's hate and from all the sorrows of life. He sat as we had left him, head bowed upon his breast; but One had come to him in the darkness, and, though all his bones were broken, he seemed like a drowned man.

Then stark horror fell like a thick fog on Faring town. We clustered about the stocks, struck silent, till shrieks from a house on the outskirts of the village told us that the horror had struck again, and, rushing there, we found red destruction and death. And a maniac woman who whimpered before she died that Adam Falcon's corpse had broken through the window, flaming-eyed and horrible, to rend and slay. A green slime fouled the room and fragments of seaweed clung to the window sill.

Then fear, unreasoning and shameless, took possession of the men of Faring town, and they fled to their separate houses, where they locked and bolted doors and windows and crouched behind them, weapons trembling in their hands and black terror in their souls. For what weapon can slay the dead?

And through the deathly night, horror stalked through Faring town and hunted the sons of men. Men shuddered and dared not even look forth when the crash of a door or window told of the entrance of the fiend into some wretch's cottage, when shrieks and gibberings told of its grisly deeds therein.

Yet there was one man who did not shut himself behind doors to be there slaughtered like a sheep. I was never a brave man. nor was it courage that sent me out into the ghostly night. No, it was the driving power of a Thought, a Thought which had birth in my brain as I looked on the dead face of Michael Hansen. A vague and illusive thing it was, a hovering and an almost-being—but not quite. Somewhere at the back of my skull it lurked, and I could not rest until I had proved or disproved that which I could not even formulate into a concrete theory.

So, with my brain in strange and chaotic condition, I stole through the shadows, warily. Mayhap the sea, strange and fickle even to her chosen, had whispered something to my inner mind, had betrayed her own. I know not.

But all through the dark hours I prowled along the beach, and, when in the first gray light of the early dawn, a fiendish shape came striding down to the shore, I was waiting there.

To all seeming it was Adam Falcon's corpse, animated by some horrid life, which fronted me there in the gray gloom. The eyes were open now, and they glimmered with a cold light, like the reflections of some deep sea hell. And I knew that it was not Adam Falcon who faced me.

"Sea fiend," I said in an unsteady voice, "I know not how you came by Adam Falcon's apparel. I know not whether his ship went upon the rocks, or whether he fell overboard, or whether you climbed up the strake and over the rail and dragged him from his own deck. Nor do I know by what foul ocean magic you twisted your devil's features into a likeness of his.

"But this I know. Adam Falcon sleeps in peace beneath the blue tides. You are not he. That I suspected—now I know. This horror has come upon Earth of yore—so long ago that all men have forgotten the tales; all except such as I, whom men name fool. I know, and knowing, I fear you not, and here I slay you, for though you are not human, you may be slain by a man who does not fear you—even though that man be only a youth and considered strange and foolish. You have left your demon's mark upon the land; God alone knows how many souls you have reft, how many brains you have shattered this night. The ancients said your kind could do harm only in the form of men, on land. Aye, you tricked the sons of men—were borne into their midst by kind and gentle hands—by men who knew not they carried a monster from the abysses.

"Now, you have worked your will, and the sun will soon rise. Before that time you must be far below the green waters, basking in the accursed caverns that human eye has never looked upon save in death. There lies the sea and safety; I alone bar the way."

He came upon me like a towering wave, and his arms were like green serpents about me. I knew they were crushing me; yet I felt as if I were drowning instead, and even then understood the expression that had puzzled me on Michael Hansen's face—that of a drowned man.

I was looking in the inhuman eyes of the monster, and it was as if I gazed into untold depths of oceans—depths into which I should presently tumble and drown. And I felt scales .

Neck, arm, and shoulder he gripped me, bending me back to break my spine, and I drove my knife into his body again—and again and again. He roared once, the only sound I ever heard him make, and it was like the roar of the tides among the shoals. Like the pressure of a hundred fathoms of green water was the grasp upon my body and limbs, and then, as I thrust again, he gave way and crumpled to the beach.

He lay there writhing and then was still, and already he had begun to change. Merman, the ancients named his kind, knowing they were endowed with strange attributes, one of which was the ability to take the full form of a man if lifted from the ocean by the hands of men. I bent and tore the human clothing from the thing And the first gleams of the sun fell upon a slimy and moldering mass of seaweed, from which stared two hideous dead eyes—a formless bulk that lay at the water's edge, where the first high wave would bear it back to that from which it came: the cold jade ocean deeps.

Robert Bloch encouraged fellow Milwaukeean, Earl Pierce Jr., into submitting several stories to WEIRD TALES. While not up to the level of Bloch's writings, the Pierce stories are all quite good. "Doom of the House of Duryea" is a powerful tale of vampirism that might just catch you by surprise.

DOOM OF THE HOUSE OF DURYEA

Earl Pierce, Jr.

Arthur Duryea, a young, handsome man, came to meet his father for the first time in twenty years. As he strode into the hotel lobby—long strides which had the spring of elastic in them—idle eyes lifted to appraise him, for he was an impressive figure, somehow grim with exaltation.

The desk clerk looked up with his habitual smile of expectation; how-do-you-do-Mr.-so-and-so, and his fingers strayed to the green fountain pen which stood in a holder on the desk.

Arthur Duryea cleared his throat, but still his voice was clogged and unsteady. To the clerk he said:

"I'm looking for my father, Doctor Henry Duryea. I understand he is registered here. He has recently arrived from Paris."

The clerk lowered his glance to a list of names. "Doctor Duryea is in suite 600, sixth floor." He looked up, his eyebrows arched questioningly. "Are you staying too, sir, Mr. Duryea?"

Arthur took the pen and scribbled his name rapidly. Without a further word, neglecting even to get his key and own room number, he turned and walked to the elevators. Not until he reached his father's suite on the sixth floor did he make an audible noise, and this was a mere sigh which fell from his lips like a prayer.

The man who opened the door was unusually tall, his slender frame clothed in tight-fitting black. He hardly dared to smile. His clean-shaven face was pale, an almost livid whiteness against the sparkle in his eyes. His jaw had a bluish luster.

"Arthur!" The word was scarcely a whisper. It seemed choked up quietly, as if it had been repeated time and again on his thin lips.

Arthur Duryea felt the kindliness of those eyes go through him, and then he was in his father's embrace.

Later, when these two grown men had regained their outer calm, they closed the door and went into the drawing-room. The elder Duryea held out a humidor of fine cigars, and his hand shook so hard when he held the match that his son was forced to cup his own hands about the flame. They both had tears in their eyes, but their eyes were smiling.

Henry Duryea placed a hand on his son's shoulder. "This is the happiest day of my life," he said. "You can never know how much I have longed for this moment."

Arthur, looking into that glance, realized, with growing pride, that he had loved his father all his life, despite any of those things which had been cursed against him. He sat down on the edge of a chair.

"I—I don't know how to act," he confessed. "You surprise me, Dad. You're so different from what I had expected."

A cloud came over Doctor Duryea's features. "What *did* you expect, Arthur?" he demanded quickly. "An evil eye? A shaven head and knotted jowls?"

"Please, Dad—no!" Arthur's words clipped short. "I don't think I ever really visualized you. I knew you would be a splendid man. But I thought you'd look older, more like a man who has really suffered."

"I have suffered, more than I can ever describe. But seeing you again, and the prospect of spending the rest of my life with you, has more than compensated for my sorrows. Even during the twenty years we were apart I found an ironic joy in learning of your progress in college, and in your American game of football."

"Then you've been following my work?"

"Yes, Arthur; I've received monthly reports ever since you left me. From my study in Paris I've been really close to you, working out your problems as if they were my own. And now that the twenty years are completed, the ban which kept us apart is lifted for ever. From now on, son, we shall be the closest of companions—unless your Aunt Cecilia has succeeded in her terrible mission."

The mention of that name caused an unfamiliar chill to come between the two men. It stood for something, in each of them, which gnawed their minds like a malignancy. But to the younger Duryea, in his intense effort to forget the awful past, her name as well as her madness must be forgotten.

He had no wish to carry on this subject of conversation, for it betrayed an internal weakness which he hated. With forced determination, and a ludicrous lift of his eyebrows, he said.

"Cecilia is dead, and her silly superstition is dead also. From now on, Dad, we're going to enjoy life as we should. Bygones are really bygones in this case."

Doctor Duryea closed his eyes slowly, as though an exquisite pain had gone through him.

"Then you have no indignation?" he questioned. "You have none of your aunt's hatred?"

"Indignation? Hatred?" Arthur laughed aloud. "Ever since I was twelve years old I have disbelieved Cecilia's stories. I have known that those horrible things were impossible, that they belonged to the ancient category of mythology and tradition. How, then, can I be indignant, and how can I hate you? How can I do anything but recognize Cecilia for what she was—a mean, frustrated woman, cursed with an insane grudge against you and your family? I tell you, Dad, that nothing she has ever said can possibly come between us again."

Henry Duryea nodded his head. His lips were tight together, and the muscles in his throat held back a cry. In that same soft tone of defense he spoke further, doubting words.

"Are you so sure of your subconscious mind, Arthur? Can you be so certain that you are free from all suspicion, however vague? Is there not a lingering premonition—a premonition which warns of peril?"

"No, Dad—no!" Arthur shot to his feet. "I don't believe it. I've never believed it. I know, as any sane man would know, that you are neither a vampire nor a murderer. You know it, too; and Cecilia knew it, only she was mad.

"That family rot is dispelled, Father. This is a civilized century. Belief in vampirism is sheer lunacy. Wh-why, it's too absurd even to think about!"

"You have the enthusiasm of youth," said his father, in a rather tired voice. "But have you not heard the legend?"

Arthur stepped back instinctively. He moistened his lips, for their dryness might crack them. "The legend?"

He said the word in a curious hush of awed softness, as he had heard his Aunt Cecilia say it many times before.

"That awful legend that you—"

"That I *eat* my children?"

"Oh, God, Father!" Arthur went to his knees as a cry burst through his lips. "Dad, that—that's ghastly! We must forget Cecilia's ravings."

"You are affected, then?" asked Doctor Duryea bitterly.

"Affected? Certainly I'm affected, but only as I should be at such an accusation. Cecilia was mad, I tell you. Those books she showed me years ago, and those folk-tales of vampires and ghouls—they burned into my infantile mind like acid. They haunted me day and night in my youth, and caused me to hate you worse than death itself.

"But in Heaven's name, Father, I've outgrown those things as I have outgrown my clothes. I'm a man now; do you understand that? A man, with a man's sense of logic."

"Yes, I understand." Henry Duryea threw his cigar into the fireplace, and placed a hand on his son's shoulder.

"We shall forget Cecilia," he said. "As I told you in my letter, I have rented a lodge in Maine where we can go to be alone for the rest of the summer. We'll get in some fishing and hiking and perhaps some hunting. But first, Arthur, I must be sure in my own mind that you are sure in yours. I must be sure you won't bar your door against me at night, and sleep with a loaded revolver at your elbow. I must be sure that you're not afraid of going up there alone with me, and dying—"

His voice ended abruptly, as if an age-long dread had taken hold of it. His son's face was waxen, with sweat standing out like pearls on his brow. He said nothing, but his eyes were filled with questions which his lips could not put into words. His own hand touched his father's, and tightened over it.

Henry Duryea drew his hand away.

"I'm sorry," he said, and his eyes looked straight over Arthur's lowered head. "This thing must be thrashed out now. I believe you when you say that you discredit Cecilia's stories, but for a sake greater than sanity I must tell you the truth behind the legend—and believe me, Arthur; there is a truth!"

He climbed to his feet and walked to the window which looked out over the street below. For a moment he gazed into space, silent. Then he turned and looked down at his son.

"You have heard only your aunt's version of the legend, Arthur. Doubtless it was warped into a thing far more hideous than it actually was—if that is possible! Doubtless she spoke to you of the Inquisitorial stake in Carcassonne where one of my ancestors perished. Also she may have mentioned that book, *Vampyrs*, which a former Duryea is supposed to have written. Then certainly she told you about your two younger brothers—my own poor, motherless children—who were sucked bloodless in their cradles. . . ."

Arthur Duryea passed a hand across his aching eyes. Those words, so often repeated by that witch of an aunt, stirred up the same visions which had made his childhood nights sleepless with terror. He could hardly bear to hear them again—and from the very man to whom they were accredited.

"Listen, Arthur," the elder Duryea went on quickly, his voice low with the pain it gave him. "You must know that true basis to your aunt's hatred. You must know of that curse—that curse of vampirism which is supposed to have followed the Duryeas through five centuries of French history, but which we can dispel as pure superstition, so often connected with ancient families. But I must tell you that this part of the legend is true:

"Your two young brothers actually died in their cradles, bloodless.

And I stood trial in France for their murder, and my name was smirched throughout all of Europe with such an inhuman damnation that it drove your aunt and you to America, and has left me childless, hated, and ostracized from society the world over.

"I must tell you that on that terrible night in Duryea Castle I had been working late on historic volumes of Crespet and Prinn, and on that loathsome tome, *Vampyrs*. I must tell you of the soreness that was in my throat and of the heaviness of the blood which coursed through my veins. . . .And of that *presence*, which was neither man nor animal, but which I knew was some place near me, yet neither within the castle nor outside of it, and which was closer to me than my heart and more terrible to me than the touch of the grave. . . .

"I was at the desk in my library, my head swimming in a delirium which left me senseless until dawn. There were nightmares that frightened me—frightened *me*, Arthur, a grown man who had dissected countless cadavers in morgues and medical schools. I know that my tongue was swollen in my mouth and that brine moistened my lips, and that a rottenness pervaded my body like a fever.

"I can make no recollection of sanity or of consciousness. That night remains vivid, unforgettable, yet somehow completely in shadows. When I had fallen asleep—if in God's name it *was* sleep—I was slumped across my desk. But when I awoke in the morning I was lying face down on my couch. So you see, Arthur, I *had* moved during that night, *and I had never known it!*

"What I'd done and where I'd gone during those dark hours will always remain an impenetrable mystery. But I do know this. On the morrow I was torn from my sleep by the shrieks of maids and butlers, and by that mad wailing of your aunt. I stumbled through the open door of my study, and in the nursery I saw those two babies there— lifeless, white and dry like mummies, and with twin holes in their necks that were caked black with their own blood. . . .

"Oh, I don't blame you for your incredulousness, Arthur. I cannot believe it yet myself, nor shall I ever believe it. The belief of it would drive me to suicide; and still the doubting of it drives me mad with horror.

"All of France was doubtful, and even the savants who defended my name at the trial found that they could not explain it nor disbelieve it. The case was quieted by the Republic, for it might have shaken science to its very foundation and split the pedestals of religion and logic. I was released from the charge of murder; but the actual murder has hung about me like a stench.

"The coroners who examined those tiny cadavers found them both dry of all their blood, but could find no blood on the floor of the nursery nor in the cradles. Something from hell stalked the halls of Duryea that night—and I should blow my brains out if I dared to think deeply of who that was. You, too, my son, would have been dead and bloodless if you hadn't been sleeping in a separate room with your door barred on the inside.

"You were a timid child, Arthur. You were only seven years old, but you were filled with the folk-lore of those mad Lombards and the decadent poetry of your aunt. On that same night, while I was some place between heaven and hell, you, also, heard the padded footsteps on the stone corridor and heard the tugging at your door handle, for in the morning you complained of a chill and of terrible nightmares which frightened you in your sleep. . . . I only thank God that your door was barred!"

Henry Duryea's voice choked into a sob which brought the stinging tears back into his eyes. He paused to wipe his face, and to dig his fingers into his palm.

"You understand, Arthur, that for twenty years, under my sworn oath at the Palace of Justice, I could neither see you nor write to you. Twenty years, my son, while all of that time you had grown to hate me and to spit at my name. Not until your aunt's death have you called yourself a Duryea. . . . And now you come to me at my bidding, and say you love me as a son should love his father.

"Perhaps it is God's forgiveness for everything. Now, at last, we shall be together, and that terrible, unexplainable past will be buried for ever. . . ."

He put his handkerchief back into his pocket and walked slowly to his son. He dropped to one knee, and his hands gripped Arthur's arms.

"My son, I can say no more to you. I have told you the truth as I alone know it. I may be, by all accounts, some ghoulish creation of Satan on earth. I may be a child-killer, a vampire, some morbidly diseased specimen of *vrykolakas*—things which science cannot explain.

"Perhaps the dreaded legend of the Duryeas is true. Autiel Duryea was convicted of murdering his brother in that same monstrous fashion in the year 1576, and he died in flames at the stake. Francois Duryea, in 1802, blew his head apart with a blunderbuss on the morning after his youngest son was found dead, apparently from anemia. And there are others, of whom I cannot bear to speak, that would chill your soul if you were to hear them.

"So you see, Arthur, there is a hellish tradition behind our family. There is a heritage which no sane God would ever have allowed. The future of the Duryeas lies in you, for you are the last of the race. I

pray with all of my heart that providence will permit you to live your
full share of years, and to leave other Duryeas behind you. And so if
ever again I feel that presence as I did in Duryea Castle, I am going
to die as Francois Duryea died, over a hundred years ago. . . ."

He stood up, and his son stood up at his side.

"If you are willing to forget, Arthur, we shall go up to that lodge
in Maine. There is a life we've never known awaiting us. We must find
that life, and we must find the happiness which a curious fate snatched
from us on those Lombard sourlands, twenty years ago. . . ."

Henry Duryea's tall stature, coupled with a slenderness of frame and
a sleekness of muscle, gave him an appearance that was unusually *gaunt*.
His son couldn't help but think of that word as he sat on the rustic
porch of the lodge, watching his father sunning himself at the lake's
edge.

Henry Duryea had a kindliness in his face, at times an almost sub-
lime kindliness which great prophets often possess. But when his face was
partly in shadows, particularly about his brow, there was a frightening
tone which came into his features; for it was a tone of farness, of mys-
ticism and conjuration. Somehow, in the late evenings, he assumed the
unapproachable mantle of a dreamer and sat silently before the fire, his
mind ever off in unknown places.

In that little lodge there was no electricity, and the glow of the oil
lamps played curious tricks with the human expression which frequently
resulted in something unhuman. It may have been the dusk of night,
the flickering of the lamps, but Arthur Duryea had certainly noticed how
his father's eyes had sunken further into his head, and how his cheeks
were tighter, and the outline of his teeth pressed into the skin about his
lips.

It was nearing sundown on the second day of their stay at Timber
Lake. Six miles away the dirt road wound on toward Houtlon, near the
Canadian border. So it was lonely there, on a solitary little lake hemmed
in closely with dark evergreens and a sky which drooped low over dusty-
summited mountains.

Within the lodge was a homy fireplace, and a glossy elk's-head which
peered out above the mantel. There were guns and fishing-tackle on the
walls, shelves of reliable American fiction—Mark Twain, Melville, Stock-
ton, and a well-worn edition of Bret Harte.

A fully supplied kitchen and a wood stove furnished them with hearty
meals which were welcome after a whole day's tramp in the woods. On
that evening Henry Duryea prepared a select French stew out of every

available vegetable, and a can of soup. They ate well, then stretched out before the fire for a smoke. They were outlining a trip to the Orient together, when the back door blew open with a terrific bang, and a wind swept into the lodge with a coldness which chilled them both.

"A storm," Henry Duryea said, rising to his feet. "Sometimes they have them up here, and they're pretty bad. The roof might leak over your bedroom. Perhaps you'd like to sleep down here with me." His fingers strayed playfully over his son's head as he went out into the kitchen to bar the swinging door.

Arthur's room was upstairs, next to a spare room filled with extra furniture. He'd chosen it because he liked the altitude, and because the only other bedroom was occupied. . . .

He went upstairs swiftly and silently. His roof didn't leak; it was absurd even to think it might. It had been his father again, suggesting that they sleep together. He had done it before, in a jesting, whispering way—as if to challenge them both if they *dared* to sleep together.

Arthur came back downstairs dressed in his bath-robe and slippers. He stood on the fifth stair, rubbing a two-day's growth of beard. "I think I'll shave tonight," he said to his father. "May I use your razor?"

Henry Duryea, draped in a black raincoat and with his face haloed in the brim of a rain-hat, looked up from the hall. A frown glided obscurely from his features. "Not at all, son. Sleeping upstairs?"

Arthur nodded, and quickly said, "Are you—going out?"

"Yes, I'm going to tie the boats up tighter. I'm afraid the lake will rough it up a bit."

Duryea jerked back the door and stepped outside. The door slammed shut, and his footsteps sounded on the wood flooring of the porch.

Arthur came slowly down the remaining steps. He saw his father's figure pass across the dark rectangle of a window, saw the flash of lightning that suddenly printed his grim silhouette against the glass.

He sighed deeply, a sigh which burned in his throat; for his throat was sore and aching. Then he went into the bedroom, found the razor lying in plain view on a birch table-top.

As he reached for it, his glance fell upon his father's open Gladstone bag which rested at the foot of the bed. There was a book resting there, half hidden by a gray flannel shirt. It was a narrow yellow-bound book, oddly out of place.

Frowning, he bent down and lifted it from the bag. It was surprisingly heavy in his hands, and he noticed a faintly sickening odor of decay which drifted from it like a perfume. The title of the volume had been thumbed away into an indecipherable blur of gold letters. But pasted across the front cover was a white strip of paper, on which was typewritten the word—INFANTIPHAGI.

He flipped back the cover and ran his eyes over the title-page. The book was printed in French—an early French—yet to him wholly comprehensible. The publication date was 1580, in Caen.

Breathlessly he turned back a second page, saw a chapter headed, *Vampires.*

He slumped to one elbow across the bed. His eyes were four inches from those mildewed pages, his nostrils reeked with the stench of them.

He skipped long paragraphs of pedantic jargon on theology, he scanned brief accounts of strange, blood-eating monsters, *vrykolakes*, and leprechauns. He read of Jeanne d'Arc, of Ludvig Prinn, and muttered aloud the Latin snatches from *Episcopi.*

He passed pages in quick succession, his fingers shaking with the fear of it and his eyes hanging heavily in their sockets. He saw vague reference to "Enoch," and saw the terrible drawings by an ancient Dominican of Rome. . . .

Paragraph after paragraph he read: the horror-striking testimony of Nider's *Ant-Hill*, the testimony of people who died shrieking at the stake; the recitals of grave-tenders, of jurists and hangmen. Then unexpectedly, among all of this munimental vestige, there appeared before his eyes the name of—*Autiel Duryea;* and he stopped reading as though invisibly struck.

Thunder clapped near the lodge and rattled the window-panes. The deep rolling of bursting clouds echoed over the valley. But he heard none of it. His eyes were on those two short sentences which his father—someone—had underlined with dark red crayon.

> . . . The execution, four years ago, of Auitel Duryea does not end the
> Duryea controversy. Time alone can decide whether the Demon has
> claimed that family from its beginning to its end . . . .

Arthur read on about the trial of Autiel Duryea before Veniti, the Carcassonnean Inquisitor-General; read, with mounting horror, the evidence which had sent that far-gone Duryea to the pillar—the evidence of a bloodless corpse who had been Autiel Duryea's young brother.

Unmindful now of the tremendous storm which had centered over Timber Lake, unheeding the clatter of windows and the swish of pines on the roof—even of his father who worked down at the lake's edge in a drenching rain—Arthur fastened his glance to the blurred print of those pages, sinking deeper and deeper into the garbled legends of a dark age. . . .

On the last page of the chapter he again saw the name of his ancestor, Autiel Duryea. He traced a shaking finger over the narrow lines of words, and when he finished reading them he rolled sideways on the bed, and from his lips came a sobbing, mumbling prayer.

"God, oh God in Heaven protect me. . . ."

For he had read:

> As in the case of Autiel Duryea we observe that this specimen of *vrykolakas* preys only upon the blood in its own family. It possesses none of the characteristics of the undead vampire, being usually a living male person of otherwise normal appearances, unsuspecting its inherent demonism.
>
> But this *vrykolakas* cannot act according to its demoniacal possession unless it is in the presence of a second member of the same family, who acts as a medium between the man and its demon. This medium has none of the traits of the vampire, but it senses the being of this creature (when the metamorphosis is about to occur) by reason of intense pains in the head and throat. Both the vampire and the medium undergo similar reactions, involving nausea, nocturnal visions, and physical disquietude.
>
> When these two outcasts are within a certain distance of each other, the coalescence of inherent demonism is completed, and the vampire is subject to its attacks, demanding blood for its sustenance. No member of the family is safe at these times, for the *vrykolakas*, acting in its true agency on earth, will unerringly seek out the blood. In rare cases, where other victims are unavailable, *the vampire will even take the blood from the very medium which made it possible.*
>
> This vampire is born into certain aged families, and naught but death can destroy it. It is not conscious of its blood-madness, and acts only in a psychic state. The medium, also, is unaware of its terrible role; and when these two are together despite any lapse of years, the fusion of inheritance is so violent that no power known on earth can turn it back.

The lodge door slammed shut with a sudden, interrupting bang. The lock grated, and Henry Duryea's footsteps sounded on the planked floor.

Arthur shook himself from the bed. He had only time to fling that haunting book into the Gladstone bag before he sensed his father standing in the doorway.

"You—you're not shaving, Arthur." Duryea's words, spliced hesitantly, were toneless. He glanced from the table-top to the Gladstone, and to his son. He said nothing for a moment, his glance inscrutable. Then,

"It's blowing up quite a storm outside."

Arthur swallowed the first words which had come into his throat, nodded quickly. "Yes, isn't it? Quite a storm." He met his father's gaze, his face burning. "I—I don't think I'll shave, Dad. My head aches."

Duryea came swiftly into the room and pinned Arthur's arms in his grasp. "What do you mean—your head aches? How? Does your throat—"

"No!" Arthur jerked himself away. He laughed. "It's that French stew of yours! It's hit me in the stomach!" He stepped past his father and started up the stairs.

"The stew?" Duryea pivoted on his heel. "Possibly. I think I feel it myself."

Arthur stopped, his face suddenly white. "You—too?"

The words were hardly audible. Their glances met—clashed like dueling-swords.

For ten seconds neither of them said a word or moved a muscle: Arthur, from the stairs, looking down; his father below, gazing up at him. In Henry Duryea the blood drained slowly from his face and left a purple etching across the bridge of his nose and above his eyes. He looked like a death's-head.

Arthur winced at the sight and twisted his eyes away. He turned to go up the remaining stairs.

"Son!"

He stopped again; his hand tightened on the banister.

"Yes, Dad?"

Duryea put his foot on the first stair. "I want you to lock your door tonight. The wind would keep it banging!"

"Yes," breathed Arthur, and pushed up the stairs to his room.

Doctor Duryea's hollow footsteps sounded in steady, unhesitant beats across the floor of Timber Lake Lodge. Sometimes they stopped, and the crackling hiss of a sulfur match took their place, then perhaps a distended sigh, and, again, footsteps. . . .

Arthur crouched at the open door of his room. His head was cocked for those noises from below. In his hands was a double-barrel shotgun of violent gage. . . .thud . . . thud . . . thud . . .

Then a pause, the clinking of a glass and the gurgling of liquid. The sign, the tread of his feet over the floor. . . .

"He's thirsty," Arthur thought—*Thirsty!*

Outside, the storm had grown into fury. Lightning zigzagged between the mountains, filling the valley with weird phosphorescence. Thunder, like drums, rolled incessantly.

Within the lodge the heat of the fireplace piled the atmosphere thick with stagnation. All the doors and windows were locked shut, the oil-lamps glowed weakly—a pale, anemic light.

Henry Duryea walked to the foot of the stairs and stood looking up.

Arthur sensed his movements and ducked back into his room, the gun gripped in his shaking fingers.

Then Henry Duryea's footstep sounded on the first stair.

Arthur slumped to one knee. He buckled a fist against his teeth as a prayer tumbled through them.

Duryea climbed a second step . . . and another . . . .and still one more. On the fourth stair he stopped.

"Arthur!" His voice cut into the silence like the crack of a whip. "Arthur! Will you come down here?"

"Yes, Dad." Bedraggled, his body hanging like cloth, young Duryea took five steps to the landing.

"We can't be zanies!" cried Henry Duryea. "My soul is sick with dread. Tomorrow we're going back to New York. I'm going to get the first boat to open sea. . . . Please come down here." He turned about and descended the stairs to his room.

Arthur choked back the words which had lumped in his mouth. Half dazed, he followed. . . .

In the bedroom he saw his father stretched face-up along the bed. He saw a pile of rope at his father's feet.

"Tie me to the bedposts, Arthur," came the command. "Tie both my hands and both my feet."

Arthur stood gaping.

"Do as I tell you!"

"Dad, what hor—"

"Don't be a fool! You read that book! You know what relation you are to me! I'd always hoped it was Cecilia, but now I know it's you. I should have known it on that night twenty years ago when you complained of a headache and nightmares. . . . Quickly, my head rocks with pain. *Tie me!*"

Speechless, his own pain piercing him with agony, Arthur fell to that grisly task. Both hands he tied—and both feet . . . tied them so firmly to the iron posts that his father could not lift himself an inch off the bed.

Then he blew out the lamps, and without a further glance at that Prometheus, he reascended the stairs to his room, and slammed and locked his door behind him.

He looked once at the breech of his gun, and set it against a chair by his bed. He flung off his robe and slippers, and within five minutes he was senseless in slumber.

He slept late, and when he awakened his muscles were as stiff as boards, and the lingering visions of a nightmare clung before his eyes. He pushed his way out of bed, stood dazedly on the floor.

A dull, numbing cruciation circulated through his head. He felt bloated . . . coarse and running with internal mucus. His mouth was dry, his gums sore and stinging.

He tightened his hands as he lunged for the door. "Dad," he cried, and he heard his voice breaking in his throat.

Sunlight filtered through the window at the top of the stairs. The air was hot and dry, and carried in it a mild odor of decay.

Arthur suddenly drew back at that odor—drew back with a gasp of awful fear. For he recognized it—that stench, the heaviness of his blood, the rawness of his tongue and gums. . . . Age-long it seemed, yet rising like a spirit in his memory. All of these things he had known and felt before.

He leaned against the banister, and half slid, half stumbled down the stairs. . . .

His father had died during the night. He lay like a waxen figure tied to his bed, his face done up in knots.

Arthur stood dumbly at the foot of the bed for only a few seconds; then he went back upstairs to his room.

Almost immediately he emptied both barrels of the shotgun into his head.

The tragedy at Timber Lake was discovered accidentally three days later. A party of fishermen, upon finding the two bodies, notified state authorities, and an investigation was directly under way.

Arthur Duryea had undoubtedly met death at his own hands. The condition of his wounds, and the manner with which he held the lethal weapon, at once foreclosed the suspicion of any foul play.

But the death of Doctor Henry Duryea confronted the police with an inexplicable mystery; for his trussed-up body, unscathed except for two jagged holes over the jugular vein, *had been drained of all its blood.*

The autopsy protocol of Henry Duryea laid death to "undetermined causes," and it was not until the yellow tabloids commenced an investigation into the Duryea family history that the incredible and fantastic explanations were offered to the public.

Obviously such talk was held in popular contempt; yet in view of the controversial war which followed, the authorities considered it expedient to consign both Duryeas to the crematory. . . . . .

*Jules de Grandin, psychic sleuth extraordinary, appeared in 93 ad-
ventures in WEIRD TALES, making him easily the most popular
character ever to appear in the magazine. In the past few years there
has been a hardcover collection of de Grandin stories as well as a
revival of several early stories in reprint magazines during the late
sixties. However, this story surprisingly remained unreprinted. Surprisingly, as in the opinion of many Quinn fans, it is the best of the
series. Here, for a change, is a menace that finds even the usually
confident Frenchman doubtful of the final outcome.*

THE CHAPEL OF MYSTIC HORROR
Seabury Quinn

I

The wind was blowing half a gale and little spits of sudden snow were
whirling through the gray November twilight as we alighted from the
accommodation train and looked expectantly up and down the uncovered
way-station platform. "Seasonable weather for Thanksgiving," I murmured, setting my face against the howling blast and making for the glowing
disk of the station-master's light.

"*Barbe d'un pelican, yes!*" assented Jules de Grandin, sinking his chin
an inch or so lower in the fur collar of his overcoat. "A polar bear
might give thanks for a warm fireside on such a night!"

"Trowbridge—I say there—Trowbridge!" a voice hailed from the
lee side of the little red-brick depot as my friend Tandy Van Riper
stepped forward, waving a welcoming hand. "This way, old-timer;
the car's waiting—so's dinner.

"Glad to meet you, Dr. de Grandin," he acknowledged as I presented the little Frenchman; "it was mighty good of you to come out
with Trowbridge and help us light the hearth fires at the Cloisters."

"Ah, then it is a new house that you have, Monsieur?" de Gradin
asked as he dropped into a seat in Van Riper's luxurious roadster and
tucked the bearskin rug snugly about his knees.

"Well, yes and no," our host replied. "The house has been up—
in America—for something like eight years, I believe, but it's new to
us. We've been in residence just a little over a month, and we're giving
a regular old-fashioned Thanksgiving party by way of housewarming."

"U'm," the Frenchman nodded thoughtfully. "Your pardon, Monsieur, it is perhaps that I do not speak the American well, but did
you not say the new house had been up in this country for only eight
years? I fear I do not apprehend. Is it that the house stood elsewhere

111

before being erected here?''

"Precisely," Van Riper agreed with a laugh. "The Cloisters were built or rebuilt, I suppose you'd say—by Miles Batterman shortly after the close of the World War. Batterman made a potful of money during the war, and a lot more in lucky speculations between the Armistice and the Treaty of Versailles. I reckon he didn't know just what to do with it all, so he blew in a couple of hundred thousand on an old Cyprian villa, had it taken down stone by stone, shipped over here, and re-erected. The building was a sort of remodeled monastery, I believe, and took Batterman's eye while he was cruising about the Mediterranean in '20. He went to a lot of trouble having it moved here and put up, and everything about the place is exactly as it was in Cyprus, except the heating and plumbing, which he added as a sort of afterthought. Quaint idea, wasn't it?''

"Decidedly," the Frenchman agreed. "And this Monsieur Batterman, did he so soon tire of his expensive toy?''

"Humph, not exactly. I got it from the administrators. I couldn't have afforded to pay a quarter the price Batterman spent on the place, let alone give him a profit on the transaction, but the fact is the old boy dropped off suddenly a year or so ago—so did his wife and daughter. The doctors said they died from eating toadstools by mistake for mushrooms. Whatever the cause was, the whole family died in a single night and the property would have gone to the State by escheat if the lawyers hadn't dug up some ninety-second cousins in Omaha. We bought the house at a public auction for about a tenth its value, and I'm figuring on holding it for a while. It'll be novel, living in a place the Knights Templar once occupied, eh?''

"Very novel—very novel, indeed, Monsieur," de Grandin replied in a queer, flat voice. "You say the Knights of the Temple once occupied this house?''

"So they tell me—some of their old furniture's still in it.''

De Grandin made an odd sound in his throat, and I turned quickly to look at him, but his face was as set and expressionless as the features of a Japanese Buddha, and if the half-smothered exclamation had been meant for conversation, he had evidently thought better of it, for he sat in stony silence during the rest of the drive.

The snow squalls had stopped by the time we drew up at the house, but the wind had increased in velocity, and in the zenith we could see the gibbous moon buffeted about in a surf of windblown clouds. Against the background of the winter sky the irregular outline of the Cloisters loomed in a forbidding silhouette. It was a high, rambling pile of gray masonry in which the characteristics of Romanesque, Gothic and Byzantine architecture were oddly blended. The walls were strengthened by a series of buttresses, crenelated with battlements and punctuated here and there with small, cylindrical watch-towers; the windows were mere slits between the great stones, and the massive entrance-way seemed fitted for a portcullis, yet a great, hemispherical dome rose from the center of the building, and a wide, shallow portico with graceful, fluted columns topped by Doric capitals stood before the gateway.

Cocktail hour had just struck as we passed through the wide entrance to the main hall, and a party of sleek-haired gentlemen and ladies in fashionably scanty attire were gathered before the cavernous fireplace, chatting and laughing as they imbibed the appetite-whetting amber drinks.

It was an enormous apartment, that hall, clear fifty feet from tiled floor to vaulted ceiling, and the darkness was scarcely more than stained by the flickering glow of blazing logs in the fireplace and the yellow beams of the tall, ecclesiastical candles which stood, singly, in high, wrought-iron standards at intervals along the walls. Draped down the bare stone sides of the hall hung a pair of prodigious tapestries, companion pieces, I thought, depicting particularly gory battle scenes, and I caught a fugitive glimpse of a black-armored knight with a cross-emblazoned surtout hacking the turbaned head from a saracen, and the tag end of the Latin legend beneath—"an Majorem De Gloriam."

Piloted by our host we mounted the wide, balustraded staircase to the second of three balconies which ran round three sides of the long hall, found the big, barnlike room assigned us, changed quickly to dinner clothes, and joined the other guests in time to file through a high archway to the oak-paneled apartment where dinner was served by candle-light on a long refectory table set with the richest silver and most opulent linen I had ever seen.

Greatly to his chagrin de Grandin drew a kittenish, elderly spinster with gleaming and palpably false dentition. I was paired off with a Miss O'Shane, a tall, tawny-haired girl with tapering, statuesque limbs and long, smooth-jointed fingers, milk-white skin of the pure-bred Celt and smoldering, rebellious eyes of indeterminate color.

During the soup and fish courses she was taciturn to the point of churlishness, responding to my attempts at conversation with curt, unisyllabic replies, but as the claret glasses were filled for the roast, she turned her strange, half-resentful gaze directly on me and demanded: "Dr. Trowbridge, what do you think of this house?"

"Why—er," I temporized, scarcely knowing what to reply, "it seems rather gorgeous, but—"

"Yes," she interrupted as I paused at a loss for an exact expression, "but what?"

"Well, rather depressing—too massive and mediaeval for present-day people, if you get what I mean."

I do," she nodded almost angrily, "I most certainly do. It's beastly. I'm a painter—a painter of sorts," she hurried on as my eyes opened in astonishment at her vehemence—"and I brought along some gear to work with between times during the party. Van told me this is liberty hall, and I could do exactly as I pleased, and gave me a big room on the north side for a workshop. I've a commission I've simply got to finish in two weeks, and I began some preliminary sketches yesterday, but—" She paused taking a sip of burgundy and looking at me from the corners of her long, brooding eyes as though speculating whether or not to take me further into her confidence.

"Yes?" I prompted, assuming an air of interest.

"It's no go. Do you remember the Red King in Through the Looking Glass?"

"The Red King?" I echoed. "I'm afraid I don't quite."

"Don't you remember how Alice took the end of his pencil in her hand when he was attempting to enter a note in his diary and made him write, 'The White Knight is sliding down the poker. He balances very badly'?"

I must have looked my bewilderment, for she laughed aloud, a deep, gurgling laugh in keeping with her rich, contralto speaking voice. "Oh, I'm not a psychopathic case—I hope," she assured me, "but I'm certainly in a position to sympathize with the poor king. It's a Christmas card I'm doing— a nice, frosty, sugar-sweet Christmas card— and I'm supposed to have a Noel scene with oxen and asses and sheep standing around the manager of a chubby little naked boy, you know— quite the conventional sort of thing." She paused again and refreshed herself with a sip of wine, and I noticed that her strong, white-fingered hand trembled as she raised the glass to her lips.

My professional interest was roused. The girl was a splendid, vital animal, lean and strong as Artemis, and the pallor of her pale skin was natural, not unhealthy; yet it required no special training to see she labored under an almost crushing burden of suppressed nervousness.

"Won't it work out?" I asked soothingly.

"No!" her reply was almost explosive. "No, it won't! I can block in the interior, all right, though it doesn't look much like a stable; but when it comes to the figures, something outside me—behind me, like Alice behind the Red King, you know, and just as invisible—seems to snatch the end of my charcoal and guide it. I keep drawing—"

Another pause broke her recital.

"Drawing what, if you please, Mademoiselle?" De Grandin turned from his partner who was in the midst of recounting a risque anecdote and leaned forward, his narrow eyebrows elevated in twin arches, his little, round blue eyes fixed and unwinking in a direct, questioning stare.

The girl started at his query. "Oh, all manner of things," she began, then broke off with a sharp, half-hysterical laugh. "Just what the Red King said when his pencil wouldn't work!" she shrilled.

For a moment I thought the little Frenchman would strike her, so fierce was the uncompromising gaze he bent on her; then: "Ah, bah, let us not think too much of fairy tales, pleasant or grim, if you please, Mademoiselle," he returned. "After dinner, if you will be so good, Dr. Trowbridge and I shall do ourselves the honor of inspecting these so mysterious self-dictated drawings of yours. Until then, let us consider this excellent food which the good Monsieur Van Riper has provided for us." Abruptly he turned to his neglected partner. "Yes, Mademoiselle," he murmured in his deferential, flattering manner, "and then the bishop said to the rector—?"

II

Dinner completed, we trooped into the high, balconied hall for coffee, tobacco and liqueurs. A radio, artfully disguised as a mediaeval Flemish console, squawked jazz with a sputtering obligato of static, and some of the guests danced, while the rest gathered at the rim of the pool of firelight and talked in muted voices. Somehow, the great stone house seemed to discourage frivolity by the sheer weight of its antiquity.

"Trowbridge, my friend," de Grandin whispered almost fiercely in my ear as he plucked me by the sleeve, "Mademoiselle O'Shane awaits our pleasure. Come, let us go to her studio at once before old Mere l'Oie tells me another of her so detestable stories of unvirtuous clergymen!"

Grinning as I wondered how the little Frenchman's late dinner partner would have enjoyed hearing herself referred to as Mother Goose, I followed him up the first flight of stairs, crossed the lower balcony and ascended a second stairway, narrow and steeper than the first, to the upper gallery where Miss O'Shane waited before the heavily carved door of a great, cavelike room paneled from flagstone floor to beamed ceiling with age-blackened oak wainscot. Candles seemed the only mode of illumination available in the house, and our hostess had lighted half a dozen tapers which stood so that their luminance fell directly on an oblong of eggshell bristol board anchored to her easel by thumbtacks.

"Now, here's what I started to do," she began, indicating the sketch with a long, beautifully manicured forefinger. "This was supposed to be the inside of the stable at Bethlehem, and—oh?" The short, half-choked exclamation, uttered with a puzzled, questioning rising inflection, cut short her sentence, and she stared at her handiwork as though it were something she had never seen before.

Leaning forward, I examined the embryonic picture curiously. As she had said at dinner, the interior, rough and elementary as it was, did not resemble a stable. Crude and rough it undoubtedly was, but with a rudeness unlike that of a barn. Cubic, rough-hewn stones composed the walls, and the vaulting of the concamerated roof was supported by a series of converging arches with piers based on blocks of oddly carved stone representing wide, naked feet, toes forward, standing on the crowns of hideous, gargoylish heads with half-human, half-reptilian faces which leered hellishly in mingled torment and rage beneath the pressure. In the middle foreground was a raised rectangular object which reminded me of a flat-topped sarcophagus, and beside it, slightly to the rear, there loomed the faint, spectral outline of a sinister, cowled figure with menacing, upraised hand, while in the lower foreground crouched, or rather groveled, a second figure, a long, boldly sketched female form with outstretched supplicating hands and face concealed by a cascade of downward-sweeping hair. Back of the hooded, monkish form were faint outlines of what had apparently first been meant to represent domestic animals, but I could see where later, heavier pencil strokes had changed them into human shapes resembling the cowled and hooded figure.

I shuddered involuntarily as I turned from the drawing, for not only in half-completed line and suggestive curve, but also in the intangible spirit of the thing was the suggestion of something bestial and unhallowed. Somehow, the thing seemed to suggest something revolting, something pregnant with the disgusting incongruity of a ribald song bawled in church when the Kyrie should be sung, or of rose-water sprinkled on putrefying offal.

De Grandin's slender dark brown eyebrows elevated till they almost met the shoreline of his sleeky combed fair hair, and the waxed points of his diminutive blond mustache reared upward like a pair of horns as he pursed his thin lips, but he made no verbal comment.

Not so Miss O'Shane. As though a sudden draft of air had blown through the room, she shivered, and I could see the horror with which she stared wide-eyed, at her own creation. "It wasn't like that!" she exclaimed in a thin, rasping whisper like the ghost of a scream. "I didn't do that!"

"Eh, how do you say, Mademoiselle?" de Grandin challenged,

regarding her with his unwinking cat-stare. "You would have us to understand that—"

"Yes!" She still spoke in a sort of awed, wondering whisper. "I didn't draw it that way! I blocked in the interior and made it of stone, for I was pretty sure the Holy Land stables were masonry, but I didn't draw those beastly arch-supports! They were just plain blocks of stone when I made them. I did put in the arches—not that I wanted to, but because I felt compelled to do it, but this—this is all different!" Her words trailed off till we could scarcely catch them, not because of lowered tone, but because they came higher, thinner, with each syllable. Stark, unreasoning terror had her by the throat, and it was with the utmost difficulty that she managed to breathe.

"H'm," de Grandin tweaked the pointed ends of his mustache. "Let us recapitulate, if you please, Mademoiselle: Yesterday and today you worked on this sketch? Yes? You drew what you conceived to be a Jewish stable in the days of Caesar Augustus—and what else, if you recall?"

"Just the stable and the bare outlines of the manger, then a half-completed figure which was to have been Joseph, and the faintest outlines of the animals and a kneeling figure before the cradle—I hadn't determined whether it would be male or female, or whether it would be full-draped or not, for I wasn't sure whether I'd have the Magi or the shepherds or just some of the village folk adoring the Infant, you see. I gave up working about four this afternoon, because the light was beginning to fail and because—"

"Eh bien, because of what, if you please, Mademoiselle?" the Frenchman prompted sharply as the girl dropped her recital.

"Because there seemed to be an actual physical opposition to my work—almost as if an invisible hand were gently but insistently forcing my pencil to draw things I hadn't conceived—things I was afraid to draw! Now, do you think I'm crazy?"

She paused again, breathing audibly through slightly parted lips, and I could see the swelling of her throat as she swallowed convulsively once or twice.

Ignoring her question, the little Frenchman regarded her thoughtfully a moment, then examined the drawing once more. "This who was to have been the good Saint Joseph, now," he asked softly, "was he robed after this fashion when you limned him?"

"No, I'd only roughed out the body. He had no face when I quit work."

"U'm, Mademoiselle, he is still without a face," de Grandin replied.

"Yes, but there's a place for his face in the opening of his hood, and if you look closely you can almost see his features—his eyes, especially. I can feel them on me, and they're not good. They're bad, wicked, cruel—like a snake's or a devil's. See, he's robed like a monk; I didn't draw him that way!''

De Grandin took up one of the candelabra and held it close to the picture, scanning the obscene thing with an unhurried, critical stare, then turned to us with a half-impatient shrug. "Tenez, my friends," he remarked, "I fear we make ourselves most wretchedly unhappy over a matter of small moment. Let us join the others."

III

Midnight had struck and de Grandin and I had managed to lose something like thirty dollars at the bridge tables before the company broke up for the evening.

"Do you really think that poor O'Shane girl is a little off her rocker?" I asked as we made ready for bed.

"I doubt it," he replied, as he fastened the sash of his pale lavender pajama jacket with a nervous tug; "indeed, I am inclined to believe all that she told us—and something more."

"You think it possible she could have been in a sort of day-dream while she drew those awful things, thinking all the while she was drawing a Christmas card?" I asked incredulously.

"Ah bah," he returned, as he kicked off his purple lizardskin slippers and leaped into bed, "what matters it what we think? Unless I am more mistaken than I think, we shall know with certitude before very long." And turning his back upon me, he dropped off to sleep.

I might have slept an hour, perhaps only a few minutes, when the sharp impact of an elbow against my ribs aroused me. "Eh?" I demanded, sitting up in bed and rubbing my eyes sleepily.

"Trowbridge, my friend," de Grandin's sharp whisper came through the darkness, "listen! Do you hear it?"

"Huh?" I responded, but:

"Ps-s-st!" he shut me off with a minatory hiss, and I held my peace, straining my ears through the chill November night.

At first I heard nothing but the skirling of the wind-fiends racing past the turreted walls, and the occasional creak of a rusty hinge as some door or shutter swung loose from its fastenings; then, very faint and faraway seeming, but growing in clarity as my ears became attuned to it, I caught the subdued notes of a piano played very softly.

"Come!" de Grandin breathed, slipping from the bed and donning a mauve-silk gown.

Obeying his summons, I rose and followed him on tiptoe across the balcony and down the stairs. As we descended, the music became clearer, more distinct. Someone was in the music room, touching the keys of the big grand piano with a delicate harpsichord touch. Liebestraum the composition was, and the gently struck notes fell, one after another, like drops of limpid water dripping from a moss-covered ledge into a quiet woodland pool.

"Why, it's exquisite," I began, but de Grandin's upraised hand cut short my commendation as he motioned me forward.

Seated before the piano was Dunroe O'Shane, her long, ivory fingers flitting over the ivory keys, her loosened tawny hair flowing over her uncovered white shoulders like molten bronze. From gently swelling breast to curving instep she was draped in a clinging shift of black-silk tissues which revealed the gracious curves of her pale body.

As we paused at the doorway the dulcet German air came to an abrupt ending, the girl's fingers began weaving sinuous patterns over the keys, as though she would conjure up some nether-world spirit from their pallid smoothness, and the room was suddenly filled with a libidinous, macabre theme in B minor, beautiful and seductive, but at the same time revolting. Swaying gently to the rhythm of the frenetic music, she turned her face toward us, and I saw her eyes were closed, long lashes sweeping against white cheeks, pale fine-veined lids calmly lowered.

"Why," I exclaimed softly, "why, de Grandin, she's asleep, she's—"

A quick movement of his hand stayed my words, as he stole softly across the rug-strewn floor, bent forward till his face was but a few inches from hers, and stared intently into veiled eyes. I could see the small blue veins in his temples swell and throb, and muscles of his throat bunch and contract with the physical effort he made to project his will into her consciousness. His thin, firm lips moved, forming soundless words, and one of his small, white hands rose slowly, finger-tips together, as though reeling thread from an invisible skein, paused a moment before her face, then moved slowly back, with a gliding, stroking motion.

Gradually, with a slow diminuendo, the wicked, salacious tune came to a pause, died to a thin, vibrating echo, ceased. Still with lowered lids and gently parted lips, the girl rose from the piano, wavered uncertainly a moment, then walked from the room with a slow, gliding step, her slim, naked feet passing soundlessly as a drift of air, as slowly she mounted the stairs.

Silently, in a sort of breathless wonder, I watched her disappear around the curve of the stone stairway, and was about to hazard a wandering opinion when a sharp exclamation from the Frenchman silenced me.

"Quick, my friend," he ordered, extinguishing the tall twin candles which burned beside the piano, "let us go up. Unless I am more badly mistaken than I think, there is that up there which is worth seeing!"

I followed him up the stairs, down the first gallery to the second flight, and down the upper balcony to the bare, forbidding room Miss O'Shane used as studio. "Ah," he breathed as he struck a wax match and ignited the candles before the drawingboard, "did I not say it? Parbleu, Friend Trowbridge, Mademoiselle O'Shane has indulged in more than one unconscious art this night, or Jules de Grandin is a liar!"

As the candle flames leaped to burning points in the still air of the room I started forward, then shrank back from the sketch their radiance revealed. Progress had been made on the picture since we had viewed it earlier in the evening. The hooded figure in the foreground was now clearly drawn, and it was no monk, but a steel-clad warrior with long white surtout worn over his armor and a white hood pulled forward, half concealing his thin, bearded face. But there was a face there, where there had been none before—a thin, vulpine, wicked face with set, cruel eyes which gloated on the prostrate figure before him. The upraised arm which had no hand when Miss O'Shane showed us the drawing after dinner now terminated in a mailed fist, and between the steel-sheathed fingers it held the stem of a chalice, a lovely, tulip-shaped cup of crystal, as though it would scatter its contents to the polished stone with which the picture room was paved. One other thing I noted before my glance shifted to the female figure—the long, red passion cross upon the white surtout was reversed, its long arm pointing upward, its transverse bar lowered, and even as I saw this I remembered vaguely that when knightly orders flourished it was the custom of heraldic courts thus to reverse a sir-knight's coats of arms when he was degraded from his chivalry as unworthy to maintain his traditions.

What had been the rough outlines of the manger were now firmly drawn into the representation of an altar, complete with the crucifix and tabernacle, but veiling the cross, so lightly sketched that, stare as I would, I could not make it out, was an odd-shaped, winged form, somewhat resembling a bat with outstretched wings.

Before the altar's lowest step the female figure, now drawn with the detail of an engraving, groveled starkly, chin and breasts, knees and elbows, instep and wrists pressed tightly to the stones; open, suppliant hands stretched forward, palms upward; rippling masses of hair flowing forward, like a plume of smoke blown in the wind, and obscuring the face.

And what was that upon the second step leading to the sanctuary? At first I thought it an alms-basin, but a second glance showed me it was a wide, shallow dish, and in it rested a long, curve-bladed knife, such as I had seen French butchers wear in their belts while enjoying a noonday smoke and resting for a space from their gory trade before the entrance of an abattoir.

"Good heavens!" I gasped, turning from the grisly scene with a feeling of physical sickness. "This is terrible, de Grandin! What are we going to do—?"

"Barbe et tete de Saint Denis, we do this!" he replied in a furious hissing voice. "Parbleu, shall Jules de Grandin be made a fool of twice in one night? Not if he knows it!"

Seizing a soap-rubber from the tray, he bent forward, and with half a dozen vigorous strokes reduced the picture to a meaningless smear of black and gray smudges.

"And now," he dusted his hands one against the other, as though to cleanse them of something foul, "let us to bed once more, my friend. I think we shall find something interesting to talk of tomorrow."

Shortly after breakfast next morning he found an excuse for separating Dunroe O'Shane from the rest of the company. "Will you not have pity on our loneliness, Mademoiselle?" he asked. "Here we lie, imprisoned in this great jail of a house, without so much as a radio program to cheer us through the morning hours. May we not trespass on your kindness and beg that you play for our delectation?"

"I play?" the girl answered with a half-incredulous smile. "Why, Dr. de Grandin, I don't know one note from another. I never played the piano in my life!"

"U'm?" He looked polite doubt as he twisted the ends of his mustache. "It is perhaps that I do not plead our cause fervently enough, Mademoiselle?"

"But truly, I can't play," she persisted.

"That's right, Dr. de Grandin," one of the young men chimed in. "Dunroe's a whiz at drawing, but she's absolutely tone-deaf. Can't carry a tune in a basket. I used to go to school with her, and they always gave her a job passing out programs or selling tickets when the class chorus sang."

De Grandin shot me a quick glance and shook his head warningly.

"What does it mean?" I asked as soon as we were together once more. "She declares she can't play, and her friends corroborate her, but—"

"But stranger things have happened, and, mordieu, still stranger ones will happen again, or the presentiment which I have is nothing more than the consequences of a too hearty breakfast!'' he broke in with one of his quick, elfin smiles. "Let us play the silly fool, Friend Trowbridge; let us pretend to believe that the moon is composed entirely of green cheese and that mice terrorize the pussy-cat. So doing, we shall learn more than if we attempt to appear filled with wisdom which we do not possess.''

IV

"Oh, I know what let's do!'' Miss Prettybridge, the lady of the scintillating teeth, whom de Grandin had squired to dinner the previous evening, exclaimed shortly after 10 o'clock that night. "This is such a romantic old house—I'm sure it's just full of memories. Let's have a seance!''

"Fine, splendid, capital!'' chorused a dozen voices. "Who'll be the medium? Anybody got a ouija board or a planchette table?''

"Order, order, please!'' the self-constituted chairwoman rapped peremptorily on a bridge table with her lorgnette. "I know how to do it! We'll go into the dining room and gather about the table. Then, when we've formed the mystic circle, if there are any spirits about we'll make 'em talk to us by rapping. Come on, everybody!''

"I don't think I like this,'' Miss O'Shane murmured as she laid her hand on my arm. Her usually pale face was paler still, and there was an expression of haunted fear in her eyes as she hesitated at the doorway.

"I don't care much for such nonsense myself,'' I admitted as we followed the others reluctantly into the refectory.

"Be close to me while this progresses, Friend Trowbridge,'' de Grandin whispered as he guided me to a seat beside him. "I care not much for this business of the monkey, but it may be the old she-fool yonder will serve our purpose unwittingly. The greatest danger is to Mademoiselle Dunroe. Keep watch on her.''

The candles in the dining-room wall sconces were extinguished, and with Miss Prettybridge at the head of the table, the entire company was seated at the board, each one with his hands outspread on the dark, polished oak before him, his thumbs touching lightly, his little fingers in contact with those of his neighbors to right and left.

"Spirits,'' Miss Prettybridge, in her role of priestess, threw out the customary challenge, "spirits, if you are here tonight, signify your presence by rapping once on the table.''

Thirty seconds or so elapsed without an answer to the lady's invitation. A woman half-way down the board tittered in half-hysterical embarrassment, and her neighbor silenced her with an impatient "sh-s-s-sh!" Then, distinctly as though thumped with a knuckle, the ancient table gave forth a resounding crack.

"If the spirit is a man, rap once; if a woman, twice," instructed Miss Prettybridge.

Another pause, somewhat longer, this time, then slowly, distinctly, two soft knocks from the very center of the table.

"Oh, a woman!" trilled one of the girls. "How perfectly thrilling!"

"And your name is—what?" demanded the mistress of ceremonies in a voice which trembled slightly in spite of her effort at control.

Thirteen slow, clear strokes sounded on the table, followed by one, then by eighteen, then others in series until nine distinct groups of blows were recorded.

"M-a-r-i-e-a-n-n-e Marie Anne—a French girl! exclaimed Miss Prettybridge. "Whom do you wish to speak with, Marie Anne? Rap when I come to the name as I call the roll. Dr. Trowbridge?

No response.

"Dr. de Grandin?"

A sharp, affirmative knock answered her, and the visitant was bidden to spell out her message.

Followed a rapid, telegraphic series of blows on the table, sometimes coming so quickly that it was impossible for us to decode them.

I listened as attentively as I could; so did everyone else, except Jules de Grandin. After a moment, during which his sleek blond head was thrust forward inquiringly, he turned his attention to Dunroe O'Shane.

The logs were burning low in the fireplace, but a shifting, flickering glow soaked through the darkness now and again, its red reflection lighting up the girl's face with a strange, unearthly illumination like the nimbus about the head of a saint in a medieval painting.

I felt the Frenchman's fingers stiffen against mine, and realized the cause of his tenseness as I stole a fleeting glance at Miss O'Shane. Her eyes had closed, and her red, petulant lips were lightly parted, as though in sleep. Over her small, regular features had crept a look of longing ecstasy.

Even my limited experience with psychotherapy was sufficient to tell me she was in a condition verging on hypnosis, if not actually over the borderline of consciousness, and I was about to leap from my seat with an offer of assistance when the insistent pressure of de Grandin's fingers on mine held me back. Turning toward him, I saw his head nod sharply toward the doorway behind the girl, and following his silent bidding, I cast my glance into the passageway in time to see someone slip quickly and noiselessly down the hall.

For a moment I sat in wondering silence, debating whether I had seen one of the servants creep past or whether I was the victim of an optical illusion, when my attention was suddenly compelled to a second figure, then a third, a fourth and a fifth passing the archway's opening like flashes of light against a darkened wall. My reason told me my eyes were playing pranks, for the gliding, soundless figures filing in quick procession past the proscenium of the dining-room door were tall, bearded men encased in gleaming black armor, and shrouded from shoulder to spurs in sable cloaks.

I blinked my eyes and shook my head in bewilderment, wondering if I had fallen into a momentary doze and dreamed the vision, but sharply, with theatrical suddenness, there sounded the raucous, brazen bray of a bugle, the skirling squeal of an unoiled windlass reeling out rope, the thud of a drawbridge falling into place; then, above the whistling November wind there winded another trumpet flourish and the clatter of iron-shod hooves against stone paving-blocks.

"Why, what was that?" Miss Prettybridge forgot the spirit message still being thumped out on the table and threw back her head in momentary alarm.

"Sounds like a troop of scouts out for an evening's lark," put in our host, rising from the table. "Queer they should come out here to toot their bugles, though."

"Ha, parbleu, you say rightly, my friend," de Grandin broke in, rising so suddenly that his chair tilted back and fell to the floor with a resounding crash. "It is queer, most damnably queer. "Boy scouts did you say? Pray they be not scouts of evil in search of some hapless little lad while a company of empty-headed fools sit idly by listening to the chatter of their decoy!

"Did none of you recognize the message the spirit had for me?"

We looked at him in silent astonishment as he lighted the wall-candles one after another and faced us with a countenance gone livid with fury.

"Ah bah, it is scarcely worth troubling to tell you," he cried, "but the important message the spirit had for me was a silly little nursery rhyme:

> "Great A, little a,
> Bouncing B.
> The cat's in the cupboard,
> And can't see me!

"No, the cat might not see that accursed decoy spirit, but Jules de Grandin could see the others as they slunk past the door upon their devil's work! Trowbridge, mon vieux, look to Mademoiselle O'Shane, if you will.''

Startled by his command, I turned round. Dunroe O'Shane had fallen forward across the table, her long, tawny hair freed from its restraining pins and lying about her head like a pool of liquid bronze. Her eyes were still closed, but the peaceful expression had gone from her face, and in its stead was a look of unutterable fear and loathing.

"Take her up, some of you," de Grandin almost shrieked. "Bear her to her chamber and Dr. Trowbridge and I will attend to her. Then, Monsieur Van Riper, if you will be so good, I shall ask you to lend us one of your swiftest motor cars.''

"A motor car—now?'' Van Riper's incredulous tone showed he doubted his ears.

"Precisement, Monsieur, permit that I compliment you on the excellence of your hearing,'' the Frenchman replied. "A swift motor car with plenty of fuel, if you please. There are certain medicines needed to attend this sickness of body and soul, and to strike directly at its cause, and we must have them without delay. Dr. Trowbridge will drive; you need not trouble your chauffeur to leave his bed.''

Ten minutes later, having no more idea of our destination that I had of the underlying causes of the last half hour's strange events, I sped down the turnpike, Van Riper's powerful motor warming up with every revolution, and gaining speed with every foot we traveled.

"Faster, faster, my friend,'' the little Frenchman besought as we whirled madly around a banked curve in the road and started down the two-mile straightaway with the speedometer registering sixty-five miles an hour.

Twin disks of lurid flame arose above the crest of the gradient before us, growing larger and brighter every second, and the pounding staccato of high powered motorcycles driven at top speed came to us through the shrieking wind.

I throttled down our engine to a legal speed as the State Troopers neared, but instead of rushing past they came to a halt, one on each side of us. "Where you from?'' demanded the one to our left, on whose arm a sergeant's chevrons showed.

"From Mr. Van Riper's house—the Cloisters,'' I answered. "I'm Dr. Trowbridge, of Harrisonville, and this is Dr. de Grandin. A young lady at the house had been taken ill, and we're rushing home for medicine.''

"Ump?'' the sergeant grunted. "Come from th' Cloisters, do you? Don't suppose you passed anyone on the road?''

"No—'' I began, but de Grandin leaned past me.

"For whom do you seek, mon sergent?'' he demanded.

"Night riders!" the words fairly spat from the policeman's lips. "Lot o' dam' kidnapers, sir. Old lady down th' road about five miles—name o' Stebbens—was walkin' home from a neighbor's with her grandson, a cute little lad about three years old, when a crowd o' bums came riding hell-bent for election past her, knocked her for a loop an' grabbed up the kid. Masqueraders they was—wore long black gowns, she said, an' rode on black horses. Went away whoopin' an' yellin' to each other in some foreign language, an' laughin' like a pack o' dogs. Be God, they'll laugh outa th' other side o' their dirty mouths if we catch 'em!"

"Come on, Shoup, let's roll," he ordered his companion.

The roar of their motorcycles grew fainter and fainter as they swept down the road, and in another moment we were pursuing our way toward the city, gathering speed with every turn of the wheels.

V

We had gone scarcely another mile before the slate-colored clouds which the wind had been piling together in the upper sky ripped apart and great clouds of soft, feathery snowflakes came tumbling down, blotting out the road ahead and cutting our speed to a snail's pace. It was almost graylight before we arrived at the outskirts of Harrisonville, and the snow was falling harder than ever as we headed up the main thoroughfare.

"Helas, my friend, there is not the chance of the Chinaman that we can return to the Cloisters before noon, be our luck of the best," de Grandin muttered disconsolately; "therefore I suggest that we go to your house and obtain a few hours' rest."

"But how about the medicine you wanted?" I objected. "Hadn't we better see about getting that first?"

"Non," he returned. "It will keep. The medicine I seek could not be administered before tonight—if that soon—and we can secure it later as well as now."

Rather surprised at our unheralded return, but used to the vagaries of a bachelor physician and his eccentric friend, Nora McGinnis, my housekeeper and general factotum, prepared a toothsome breakfast for us next morning, and we had completed the meal, lingering over coffee and cigarettes a little longer than usual, when de Grandin's face suddenly went livid as he thrust the folded newspaper he had been reading into my hand.

"Look, mon ami," he whispered raspingly. "Read what is there. They did not wait long to be about their deviltry!"

STATE COP DEAD IN MYSTERY KILLING

announded the headline to which he had directed my attention. Below was a brief dispatch, evidently a bit of last-minute news, sandwiched between the announcement of a sheriff's sale and a patent medicine advertisement:

Johnskill—Sergeant Rosswell of the state constabulary is dead and Private Shoup in a serious condition as the result of a battle with a mysterious band of masked ruffians near this place early this morning. Shortly after 10 o'clock last night Matilda Stebbens, of Osmondville, who was returning from a visit to a neighbor's with her three-year-old grandson, George, was attacked by a company of men mounted on black or dark-colored horses and enveloped in long black gowns, according to her story to the troopers. The leader of the gang struck her a heavy blow with a club or blackjack, evidently with the intention of stunning her and seized the little boy, lifting him to his saddle. Had it not been for the fact that Mrs. Stebbens still affects long hair and was wearing a stiff felt hat, the blow would undoubtedly have rendered her unconscious, but as it was she was merely knocked into the roadside ditch without losing consciousness, and as she lay there, half stunned from the blow, she heard the kidnapers exchange several words in some foreign language, Italian, she thought, before they set out at a break-neck pace, giving vent to wild whoops and yells. The direction of their flight was toward this place, and as soon as she was able to walk, Mrs. Stebbens hobbled to the nearest telephone and communicated with the state police.

Sergeant Rosswell and Private Shoup were detailed to the case and started in pursuit of the abductors on their motorcycles, encountering no one along the road who would admit having seen the company of mysterious mounted gangsters. About two miles this side of the Cloisters, palatial country place of Tandy Van Riper, well-known New York financier, according to Trooper Shoup, he and his companion came upon the kidnapers, riding at almost incredible speed. Drawing their pistols, the state policemen, called on the fleeing men to halt, and receiving no reply, opened fire. Their bullets, though fired at almost point-blank range, seemed to take no effect, Trooper Shoup declares, and the leader of the criminal band turned about and charged him and his companion, deliberately riding Sergeant Rosswell down. According to Shoup, a shot fired by Rosswell directly at the horse which was about to trample him, took no effect, though the pistol was less than three feet from the beast's breast. Shoup is suffering from a broken arm, three fractured ribs and a severe bruise on the head, which, he alleges, was dealt him when one of the thugs struck him with the flat of a sword.

Physicians at Mercy Hospital, believing Shoup's description of the criminals and the fight to be colored by the beating he received, intimate that he is not wholly responsible for his statements, as he positively declares that every member of the band of criminals was fully arrayed in black armor and armed with a long sword.

Working on the theory that the kidnapers are a band of Italian desperadoes who assumed this fantastic disguise, strong posses of state police are scouring the neighborhood. It is thought the little Stebbens boy was abducted by mistake, as the family are known to be in very moderate circumstances and the chances of obtaining a ransom for the lad are slight.

"You see?" de Grandin asked as I put the paper down with an exclamation of dismay.

"No, I'm hanged if I do," I shot back, "The whole gruesome business is beyond me. Is there any connection between what we saw at the Cloisters last night and—"

"*Mort d'un rat noir,* is there connection between the serpent and his venom—the Devil and the flames of hell?" he cried. "Yes, my friend, there is such a connection as will take all our skill and courage to break, I fear. Meantime, let us hasten, let us fly to the City Hospital. There is that there which shall prove more than a surprise to those vile miscreants, those forsworn servants of the Lord, when next we see them, *mon vieux.*"

"What in the world are you talking about?" I demanded. "Whom do you mean by 'forsworn servants of the Lord'?"

"Ha, good friend," he returned, his face working with emotion, "you will know in due time, if what I suspect is true. If not—" He raised his narrow shoulders in a fatalistic shrug as he snatched his overcoat.

For upward of half an hour I cooled my heels in the frosty winter air while de Grandin was closeted in conference with the superintendent of the City Hospital, but when he came out he was wearing such a smile of serene happiness that I had not the heart to berate him for leaving me outside so long.

"And now, kind friend, if you will take me so far as the pro-cathedral, I shall have done the last of my errands, and we may begin our journey to the Cloisters," he announced as he leaped nimbly into the seat beside me.

The Right Reverend De Motte Gregory, suffragan bishop of our diocese, was seated at his desk in the synod house as de Grandin and I were announced, and graciously consented to see us at once. He had been a more than ordinarily successful railway executive, a licensed legal practitioner and a certified public accountant before he assumed the cloth, and his worldly training had taught him the value of time and words, both his own and others', and rarely did he waste either.

"Monsieur l'Eveque," de Grandin began after he had greeted the gray-haired cleric with a rigidly formal European bow, "in the garden of your beautiful church there grows a bush raised from a sprig of the Holy Thorn of Glastonbury—the tree which sprang from the staff of the blessed Joseph of Arimathea when he landed in Britain after his voyage and travail. Monseigneur, we are come to beg a so little spray of that shrub from you."

The bishop's eyes opened wide with surprise, but de Grandin gave him no time for reflection.

"Sir," he hurried on, "it is not that we wish to adorn our own gardens, nor yet to put it to a shameful commercial use, but we need it—need it most urgently in a matter of great importance which is toward—"

Leaving his chair he leaned across the bishop's wide rosewood desk and began whispering rapidly in the churchman's ear.

The slightly annoyed frown which mounted to the bishop's face as the little Frenchman took the liberty changed slowly to a look of incredulity, then to an expression of amazement, "You really believe this?" he asked at length.

"More, Monseigneur, I almost know it," de Grandin assured him earnestly, "and if I am mistaken, as I hope I am but fear I am not, the holy thorn can do no harm, while it may—" He paused, waving his hand in an expressive gesture.

Bishop Gregory touched one of the row of call-buttons on his desk. "You shall have the cutting from the tree, and be very welcome," he assured my friend, "but I join with you in the hope you are mistaken."

"Grand merci, Monseigneur!" de Grandin acknowledged with another bow. "Mordieu, but your great heart is equaled only by your massive intellect! Half the clergy would have said I raved had I told them one small quarter of what I related to you."

The bishop smiled a little wearily as he put the sprig thorn-bush into de Grandin's hand. "Half the clergy, like half the laity, know so much that they know next to nothing," he replied.

"Name of a name," de Grandin swore enthusiastically as we turned toward the Cloisters, "and they say he is a wordly man! Pardieu, when will the foolish ones learn that the man who dedicates wordly wisdom to heaven's service is the most valuable servant of all?"

VI

Dunroe O'Shane was attired in a long, brown-linen smock and hard
at work on her drawing when we arrived at the Cloisters shortly before
luncheon. She seemed none the worse for her fainting fit of the previous night, and the company were rather inclined to rally de Grandin
on the serious diagnosis he had made before rushing away to secure
medicine for her.

I was amazed at the good-natured manner in which he took their
chaffing, but a hasty whisper in my ear explained his self-control.
"Apes' anger and fools' laughter are alike to be treated with scorn, my
friend," he told me. "We—you and I—have work to do here, and we
must not let the hum of pestilent gnats drive us from our purpose."

Bridge and dancing filled the evening from dinner to midnight, and
the party broke up shortly after 12 with the understanding that all were
to be ready to attend Thanksgiving services in the near-by parish church
at 11 o'clock next morning.

"Ts-s-st, Friend Trowbridge, do not disrobe," de Grandin ordered
as I was about to shed my dinner clothes and prepare for bed; "we
must be ready for an instant sortie from now until cockcrow tomorrow,
I fear."

"What's this all about, anyhow?" I demanded a little irritably, as
I dropped on the bed and wrapped myself in a blanket. "There's
been more confounded mystery here than I ever saw in a harmless old
house, what with Miss O'Shane making funny drawings, throwing
fainting-fits, and bugles sounding in the courtyard, and—"

"Ha, harmless, did you say?" he cut in with a grim smile. "My
friend, if this house be harmless, then prussic acid is a healthful drink.
Attend me with care, if you please. Do you know what this place is?"

"Certainly I do," I responded with some heat. "It's an old Cypriote
villa brought to America and—"

"It was once a chapter house of the Knights of the Temple," he
interrupted shortly, "and a Cyprian chapter house, at that. Does that
mean nothing to you? Do you not know the Knights Templars my
friend?"

"I ought to," I replied. "I've been one for the last fifteen years."

"Oh, la, la!" he laughed. "You will surely slay me, my friend.
You good, kind American gentlemen who dress in pretty uniforms and
carry swords are no more like the old Knights of the Temple of Solomon than are these other good men who wear red tarbooshes and call
themselves Nobles of the Mystic Shrine like the woman-stealing, pilgrim-

murdering Arabs of the desert.

"Listen: The history of the Templars' order is a long one, but we can touch its high spots in a few words. Formed originally for the purpose of fighting the Infidel in Palestine and aiding poor pilgrims to the Holy City they did yeomen service in the cause of God; but when Europe forsook its crusades and the Saracens took Jerusalem, the knights, whose work was done, did not disband. Not they. Instead, they clung to their various houses in Europe, and grew fat, lazy and wicked in a life of leisure, supported by the vast wealth they had amassed from gifts from grateful pilgrims and the spoils of battle. In 1191 they bought the Isle of Cyprus from Richard I of England and established several chapter houses there, and it was in those houses that unspeakable things were done. Cyprus is one of the most ancient dwelling places of religion, and of her illegitimate sister, superstition. It was there that the worshipers of Cytherea, goddess of beauty and of love—and other things less pleasant—had their stronghold. Before the Romans held the land it was drenched with unspeakable orgies. The very name of the island has passed into an invidious adjective in your language—do you not say a thing is Cyprian when you would signify it is lascivious? Certainly."

"But—"

"Hear me," he persisted, waving aside my interruption. "This Cytherea was but another form of Aphrodite, and Aphrodite, in turn, was but another name for the Eastern Goddess Astarte or Istar. You begin to comprehend? Her rites were celebrated with obscene debaucheries, but her worshipers became such human swine that only the most revolting inversions of natural things would satisfy them. The flaunting and sacrifices of virtue were not enough; they must need sacrifice—literally—those things which impersonated virtue—little, innocent children and chaste young maidens. Their foul altars must run red with the blood of innocence. These things were traditions in Cyprus long before the Knights Templars took up thir abode there, and, as one cannot sleep among dogs without acquiring fleas, so the knights, grown slothful and lazy, with nothing to do but think up ways of spending their time and wealth, became addicts to the evils of the earlier, heathen ways of their new home. Thoughts are things, my friend, and the evil thoughts of the old Cyprians took root and flourished in the brains of those unfortunate old warrior-monks whose hands were no longer busy with the sword and whose lips no longer did service to the Most High God.

"You doubt it? Consider: Though Philip IV and Clement V undoubtedly did Jacques de Molay to death for no better reason than that they might cast lots for his raiment, the fact remains that many of the knights confessed to dreadful sacrileges committed in the chapter houses—

to children slain on the altars once dedicated to God, all in the name
of the heathen goddess Cytherea.

"This very house wherein we sit was once the scene of such terrible
things as those. About its stones must linger the presence of the evil men,
the renegade priests of God, who once did them. These discarnate intelligences have lain dormant since the Fourteenth Century, but for some
reason, which we will not now discuss, I believe they have wakened into
physical beings once more. It was their reincarnated spirits we saw flitting
past the door last night while Mademoiselle Dunroe lay in a trance; it
was they who took the little boy from his grandmother's arms; it was
they who slew the brave policeman; it is they who will soon attempt to
perform the hideous inversion of the mass."

"See here, de Grandin," I expostulated, "there have been some
deucedly queer goings-on here, I'll admit, but when you try to tell me
that a lot of old soldier-monks have come to life again and are traipsing
around the countryside stealing children, you're piling it on a bit too
thick. Now, if there were any evidence to prove that—"

"Silence!" his sharp whisper brought me up with a start as he rose
from his chair and crept, catlike, toward the door, opening it a crack
and glancing down the darkened corridor outside. Then:

"Come, my friend," he bade in a low breath, "come and see what
I behold."

As he swung the door back I glanced down the long, stone-paved
gallery, dark as Erebus save as cancellated bars of moonlight shot obli-
quely down from the tiny mullioned windows piercing the dome, and
made out a gliding, wraithlike figure in trailing white garments.

"Dunroe O'Shane!" I murmured dazedly, watching the retreating
form slipping soundlessly down the dark balcony. The wavering light
of the candle she bore in her upraised hand cast gigantic shadows against
the carved balustrade and the sculptured uprights of the interlaced arches
supporting the gallery above, and hobgoblin shades seemed to march
along beside her like an escort of unclean genii from the legions of Eblis.
I watched open-mouthed with amazement as she slipped down the passage, her feet, obscured in a haze of trailing draperies, treading noiselessly, her free hand stretched outward toward the balcony rail. Next
moment the gallery was deserted; abruptly as a motion picture fades
from the screen when the projecting light winks out, Dunroe O'Shane
and her flickering rushlight vanished from our sight.

"Quick, Friend Trowbridge," the Frenchman whispered, "after her
—it was through that further door she went!"

Quietly as possible we ran down the gallery, paused before the high,
pointed-topped door and wrenched at its wrought-iron handle. The oaken

panels held firm, for the door was latched on the farther side.

"Ten thousand little devils!" de Grandin cried in vexation. "We are stalemated!"

For a moment I thought he would hurl himself against the four-inch planks of the door in impotent fury, but he collected himself with an effort, and drawing a flashlight from his jacket pocket, handed it to me with the command, "Hold the light steady on the keyhole, my friend." The next instant he sank to his knees, produced two short lengths of thin steel wire and began methodically picking the lock.

"Ha," he exclaimed, as he rose and dusted the knees of his trousers, "those old ones built for strength, Friend Trowbridge, but they knew little of subtlety. Little did that ancient locksmith dream his handiwork would one day meet with Jules de Grandin."

The unbarred door swung inward beneath his touch, and we stepped across the stone still of a vast, dungeon-dark apartment.

"Mademoiselle?" he called softly. "Mademoiselle Dunroe—are you here?"

He shot the searching beam of his flashlight hither and yon about the big room, disclosing high walls of heavy carved oak, a great canopy bed, several cathedral chairs and one or two massive, iron-bound chests—but found no living thing.

"Mordieu, but this is strange!" he muttered, sinking to his knees to flash his light beneath the high-carved bed.

"Into this room she did most certainly come but a few little minutes ago, gliding like a spirit, and now, pouf, out of this same room she does vanish like a ghost!"

Though somewhat larger, the room was similar to most other bed-chambers in the house, paneled with rather crudely carved, age-blackened wood for the entire height of its walls, ceiled with great beams which still bore the marks of the adz, and floored with octagonal marble tiles of alternate black and white. We went over every inch of it, searching for some secret exit, for, save the one by which we had entered, there was no door in the place, and the two great windows were of crude, semi-transparent glass let into metal frames securely cemented to the surround-ing stones. Plainly, nobody had left the room that way.

At the farther end of the apartment stood a stall wardrobe, elaborate-ly decorated with carved scenes of chase and battle. Opening one of the double doors letting into the press, de Grandin inspected the interior, which, like the outside was carved in every available place. "U'm?" he said, surveying the walls under his flashlight. "It may be that this is but the anteroom to—ha!"

He broke off, pointing dramatically to a carved group in the center of one of the back panels. It represented a procession of hunters returning from their sport, deer, boar and other animals lashed to long poles which the huntsmen bore shoulder-high. The men were filing through the arched entrance to a castle, the great doors of which swung back to receive them. One of the door-leaves, apparently, had warped loose from the body of the plank from which it was carved.

"*C'est tres adroit, n'est-ce-pas?*" my companion asked with a delighted grin. "Had I not seen such things before, it might have imposed on me. As it is—"

Reaching forward, he gave the loosened door a sharp, quick push, and the entire back of the wardrobe slipped upward revealing a narrow opening.

"And what have we here?" de Grandin asked, playing his spotlight through the secret doorway.

Straight ahead for three or four feet ran a flagstone sill, worn smooth in the center, as though with the shuffling tread of many feet. Beyond that began a flight of narrow, stone stairs which spiraled steeply down a shaft like the flue of a monster chimney.

De Grandin turned to me, and his little, heart-shaped face was graver than I had ever seen it.

"Trowbridge, dear, kind friend," he said in a voice so low and hoarse I could scarcely make out his words, "we have faced many perils together—perils of spirit and perils of flesh—and always we have triumphed. This time we may not. If I do not mistake rightly, there lies below these steps an evil more ancient and potent than any we have hitherto met. I have armed us against it with the weapons of religion and of science, but—I do not know that they will avail. Say, then, will you turn back now and go to your bed? I shall think no less of you, for no man should be compelled to face this thing unknowingly, and there is now no time to explain. If I survive, I shall return and tell you all. If I come not back with daylight, know that I have perished in my failure, and think kindly of me as one who loved you deeply. Will you not now say adieu, old friend?" He extended his hand and I saw the long, smooth-jointed fingers were trembling with suppressed nervousness.

"I will not!" I returned hotly, stung to the quick by his suggestion. "I don't know what's down there, but if you go, I go, too!"

Before I realized what he was about, he had flung his arms about my neck and kissed me on both cheeks. "Onward, then, brave comrade!" he cried. "This night we fight such a fight as had not been waged since the sainted George slew the monster!"

VII

Round and round a steadily descending spiral, while I counted a hundred and seventy steps, we went, going deeper into inky blackness. Finally, when I had begun to grow giddy with the endless corkscrew turns, we arrived at a steeply sloping tunnel, floored with smooth black-and-white tiles. Down this we hastened, until we traversed a distance of a hundred feet; then for a similar length we trod a level path, and began an ascent as steep as the first decline.

"Careful—cautiously, my friend," the Frenchman warned in a whisper.

Pausing a moment while he fumbled in the pocket of his jacket, my companion strode toward the barrier and laid his left hand on its heavy, wrought-iron latch.

The portal swung back almost as he touched it, and:

"*Qui va la?*" challenged a voice from the darkness.

De Grandin threw the ray of his torch across the doorway, disclosing a tall, spare form in gleaming black plate-armor over which was drawn the brown-serge habit of a monk. The sentry wore his hair in a sort of bob approximating the haircut affected by children today, and on his sallow immature face sprouted the rudiments of a straggling beard. It was a youthful face and a weak one which de Grandin's light disclosed, but the face of youth already well schooled in viciousness.

"*Qui vive?*" the fellow called doubtfully in a rather high, effeminate voice, laying a hand on the hilt of a heavy broadsword dangling from the wide, brass-studded baldric looped over his cassock.

"Those on the service of the Most High God, petit bete!" returned de Grndin, drawing something (a pronged sprig of wood, I thought) from his jacket pocket and thrusting it toward the warder's face.

"Ohe!" cried the other sharply, shrinking back. "Touch me not, good messires, I pray—I—"

"Ha—so?" de Grandin gritted between his teeth, and drew the branched stick downward across the sentry's face.

Astonishingly, the youth seemed to shrink and shrivel in upon himself. Trembling as though with an ague, he bent forward, buckled at the knees, fell toward the floor, and—was gone! Sword, armor, cassock and the man who wore them dwindled to nothingness before our sight.

A hundred feet or so farther on, our way was barred by another door, wider, higher and heavier than the first. While no tiler guarded it, it was so firmly locked that all our efforts were powerless to budge it.

"Friend Trowbridge," de Grandin announced, "it seems we shall have to pick this lock, even as we did the other. Do you keep watch through yonder grille while I make the way open for us.'' Reaching up, he moved aside a shutter covering a barred peephole in the door's thick panels; then, dropping to his knees, drew forth his wires and began working at the lock.

Gazing through the tiny wicket, I beheld a chapel-like room of circular formation, cunningly floored with slabs of polished yellow stone, inlaid with occasional plaques of purple.

By the glow of a wavering vigil lamp and the flicker of several guttering ecclesiastical candles, I saw the place was roofed with a vaulted ceiling supported by a number of converging arches, and the pier of each arch was supported by the carved image of a huge human foot which rested on the crown of a hideous, half-human head, crushing it downward and causing it to grimace hellishly with mingled pain and fury.

Beyond the yellow sanctuary lamp loomed the altar, approached by three low steps, and on it was a tall wooden crucifix from which the corpus had been stripped and to which had been nailed, in obscure caricature, a huge black bat. The staples fastening the poor beast to the cross must have hurt unmercifully, for it strove hysterically to free itself.

Almost sickened at the sight, I described the scene to de Grandin as he worked at the lock, speaking in a muted whisper, for, though there was no sign of living thing save the tortured bat, I felt that there were listening ears concealed in the darkness.

"Good!" he grunted as he hastened with his task. "It may be we are yet in time, good friend.'' Even as he spoke there came a sharp click, and the door's heavy bolts slipped back under the pressure of his improvised picklock.

Slowly, inch by careful inch, we forced the great door back.

But even as we did so, there came from the rear of the circular chamber the subdued measures of a softly intoned Gregorian chant, and something white moved forward through the shadows.

It was a man arrayed in black-steel armor over which was drawn a white surtout emblazoned with a reversed passion cross, and in his hands he bore a wide-mouthed brazen bowl like an alms-basin. In the tray rested a wicked-looking, curve-bladed knife.

With a mocking genuflection to the altar he strode up the steps and placed his burden on the second tread; then, with a coarse guffaw, he spat upon the pinioned bat and backed downward.

As a signal a double file of armored men came marching out of the gloom, ranged themselves in two ranks, one to right, one to left of the altar, and whipped their long swords from their sheaths, clashing them together, tip to tip, forming an arcade of flashing steel between them.

So softly that I felt, rather than heard him, de Grandin sighed in suppressed fury as blade met blade and two more men-at-arms, each bearing a smoking censer, strode forward beneath the roof of steel. The perfume of the incense was strong, acrid, sweet, and it mounted to our brains like the fumes of some accursed drug. But even as we sniffed its seductive scent, our eyes widened at the sight of the form which paced slowly behind the mailed acolytes.

Ceremoniously, step by pausing step, she came, like a bride marching under the arbor of uplifted swords at a military wedding, and my eyes fairly arched at the beauty of her. Milk-white, lissom and pliant as a peeled willow wand, clad only in the jeweled loveliness of her own pearly whiteness, long, bronze hair sweeping in a cloven tide from her pale brow and cataracting over her tapering shoulders, came Dunroe O'Shane. Her eyes were closed, as though in sleep, and on her red, full lips lay the yearning half-smile of the bride who ascends the aisle to meet her bridegroom, or the novice who mounts the altar steps to make her full profession. And as she advanced, her supple, long-fingered hands waved slowly to and fro, weaving fantastic arabesques in the air.

"Hail, Cytherea, Queen and Priestess and Goddess; hail, She Who Confers Life and Being on Her Servants!" came the fullthroated salutation of the double row of armored men as they clashed their blades together in martial salute, then dropped to one knee in greeting and adoration.

For a moment the undraped priestess paused below the altar stairs; then, as though forced downward by invincible pressure, she dropped, and we heard the smacking impact of soft flesh against the stone floor as she flung herself prostrate and beat her brow and hands against the floor in utter self-abasement before the marble altar and its defiled calvary.

"Is all prepared?" The question rang out sonorously as a cowled figure advanced from the shadows and strode with a swaggering step to the altar.

"All is prepared!" the congregation answered with one voice.

"Then bring the paschal lamb, even the lamb without fleece!" The deep-voiced command somehow sent shivers through me.

Two armored votaries slipped quietly away, returning in an instant with the struggling body of a little boy between them—a chubby child, naked, who fought and kicked and offered such resistance as his puny strength allowed while he called aloud to "Mamma" and "Grandma" to save him.

Down against the altar steps the butchers flung the little man; then one took his chubby, dimpled hands in relentless grip while the other drew backward at his ankles, suspending him above the wide-mouthed brazen bowl reposing on the second step.

"Take up the knife, Priestess and Queen of goodly Salamis," the hooded master of ceremonies commanded. "Take up the sacrificial knife, that the red blood may flow to our Goddess, and we hold high wassail in Her honor! O'er land and sea, o'er burning desert and heaving billow have we journeyed—"

"Villains—assassins—renegades!" Jules de Grandin bounded from his station in the shadow like a frenzied cat. "By the blood of all the blessed martyrs, you have journeyed altogether too far from hell, your home!"

"Ha? Interlopers?" rasped the hooded man. "So be it. Three hearts shall smoke upon our altar instead of one!"

"Parbleu, nothing shall smoke but the fires of your endless torture as your foul carcasses burn ceaselessly in hell!" de Grandin returned, leaping forward and drawing out the forked stick with which he had struck down the porter at the outer gate.

A burst of contemptuous laughter greeted him. "Thinkest thou to overcome me with such a toy?" the cowled one asked between shouts. "My warder at the gate succumbed to your charms—he was a poor weakling. Him you have passed, but not me. Now die!"

From beneath his cassock he snatched a long, two-handed sword, whirled its blade aloft in a triple flourish, and struck directly at de Grandin's head.

Almost by a miracle, it seemed, the Frenchman avoided the blow, dropped his useless spring of thornwood and snatched a tiny, quill-like object from his pocket. Dodging the devastating thrusts of the enemy de Grandin toyed an instant with the capsule in his hand, unscrewed the cap and, suddenly changing his tactics, advanced directly on his foe.

"Ha, Monsieur from the Fires, here is fire you know not of!" he shouted, thrusting forward the queer-looking rod and advancing within reach of the other's sword.

I stared in open-mouthed amazement. Poised for another slashing blow with his great sword, the armed man wavered momentarily, while an expression of astonishment, bewilderment, finally craven fear overspread his lean, predatory features. Lowering his sword, he thrust feebly with the point, but there was no force behind the stab; the deadly steel clattered to the floor before he could drive it into the little Frenchman's breast.

The hooded man seemed growing thinner; his tall, spare form, which had bulked a full head taller than de Grandin a moment before, seemed losing substance—growing gradually transparent, like an early morning fog slowly dissolving before the strengthening rays of the rising sun. Behind him, through him, I could dimly espy the outlines of the violated altar and the prostrate woman before its steps. Now the objects in the background became plainer and plainer. The figure of the armored man was no longer a thing of flesh and blood and cold steel overspread with a monk's habit, but an unsubstantial phantom, like an oddly shaped cloud. It was composed of trailing, rolling clouds of luminous vapor which gradually disintegrated into strands and floating webs of phosphorescence, and these, in turn, gave way to scores of little nebula of light which glowed like cigarette-ends of intense blue radiance. Then, where the nebula had been were only dancing, shifting specks of bright blue fire, finally nothing but a few pin-points of light; then—nothing.

Like shadows thrown of forest trees when the moon is at her zenith, the double row of men-at-arms stood at ease while de Grandin battled with their champion; now, their leader gone, they turned and scuttled in panic toward the rearward shadows, but Jules de Grandin was after them like a speeding arrow.

"Ha, renegades," he called mockingly, pressing closer and closer, "you who steal away helpless little by-babies from the arms of their grand'meres and then would sacrifice them on your altar, do you like the feast Jules de Grandin brings? You who would make wassail with the blood of babies—drink the draft I have prepared! Fools, mockers at God, where now is your deity? Call on her—call on Cytherea! Pardieu, I fear her not.

As it was with the master, so it was with the underlings: Closer and closer de Grandin pressed against the struggling mass of demoralized men, before his advance like ice when pressed upon by red-hot iron. One moment they milled and struggled, shrieking for aid to some unclean deity; the next they were dissolved into nebulous vapor, drifting aimlessly a moment in the still air, then swept away to nothingness.

"And so, my friend, that is done," announced de Grandin matter-of-factly as he might have mentioned the ending of a meal. "There crouches Mademoiselle O'Shane, Friend Trowbridge; come, let us seek her clothes—they should be somewhere here."

Behind the altar we found Dunroe's nightrobe and negligee lying in a ring, just as she had shrugged out of them before taking up her march between the upraised swords. Gently as a nurse attending a babe, the little Frenchman raised the swooning girl from her groveling posture before the altar, draped her robes about her, and took her in his arms.

A wailing cry, rising gradually to an incensed roar, echoed and reverberated through the vaulted chamber, and de Grandin thrust the unconscious girl into my hands. "Mon Dieu," he exclaimed, "I did forget. Le petit garcon!''

Crouched as close to the wall as he could get, we found the little lad, tears of surprising size streaming down his fat cheeks as his little mouth opened wide and emitted wail after broken-hearted wail. ''Hola, my little cabbage, mon brave soldat!'' de Grandin soothed him, stretching out his hands to the weeping youngster. ''Come with me. Come, we shall clothe you warmly against the cold and pop you into a bed of feathers, and tomorrow morning we return you to your mother's arms.''

Panting under my burden, for she was no lightweight, I bore Dunroe O'Shane up the long, tortuous flight of steps.

''Morphine is indicated here, if I do not mistake,'' de Grandin remarked as we laid the girl on her bed.

''But we haven't any—'' I began, only to be checked by his grin.

''Oh, but we have,'' he contradicted. ''I foresaw something like this was likely to come about, and abstracted a quantity of the drug, together with a syringe, from your surgery before we left home.''

When we had administered the narcotic, we set out for our own chamber, the little boy, warmly bundled in blankets, held tightly in de Grandin's arms. At a nod from the Frenchman we paused at Dunroe's studio, lighted several candles and inspected her work. Fairly spread upon her drawing-board was a pretty little scene—a dimpled little boy crowing and smiling in his mother's lap, a proud and happy father leaning over them, and in the foreground a group of rough bucolics kneeling in smiling adoration. ''Why, the influence, whatever it was, seems to have left her before we went down those secret stairs!'' I exclaimed, looking admiringly at the drawing.

''Do you say so?'' de Grandin asked as he bent closer to inspect the picture. ''Look here, if you please, my friend.''

Bringing my eyes within a few inches of the board on which the Christmas scene was sketched, I saw, so faint it was hardly to be found unless the beholder looked for it, another picture, lightly sketched in jerky, uneven lines, depicting another scene—a vaulted chapel with walls lined by armed men, two of whom held a child's body horizontally before the altar, while a woman, clothed only in her long, trailing hair, plunged a wicked, curve-bladed knife into the little one's body, piercing the heart.

''Good Lord!'' I exclaimed, in horror.

''Precisely,'' agreed Jules de Grandin. ''The good Lord inspired talent in the poor girl's hand, but the powers of darkness dictated that sketch. Perhaps—I can not say for sure—she drew both the picture we see here, and the good one was formerly the faint one, but when I overcame the wicked ones, the wicked scene faded to insignificance and the pleasing one became predominant. It is possible, and—nom d'un nom!''

"What now?'' I demanded as he turned a conscience-smitten face toward me and thrust the sleeping child into my arms.

"La chauve-souris—the bat!'' he exclaimed. "I did forget the poor one's sufferings in the stress of greater things. Take the little man to our room, and soothe him, my friend. Me, I go down those ten-thousand-times-damned stairs to that never-enough-to-be-cursed chapel and put the poor brute out of its misery!''

"You mean you're actually going into that horrible place again?'' I demanded.

"Eh bien, why not?'' he asked.

"Why—those terrible men—those—'' I began, but he stopped me.

"My friend,'' he asked as he extracted a cigarette from his dressing gown pocket and lighted it nonchalantly, "have you not yet learned that when Jules de Grandin kills a thing—be it man or be it devil—it is dead? There is nothing there which could harm a new-born fly, I do solemnly assure you.''

VIII

Jules de Grandin poured out a couple of tablespoonfuls of brandy into a wide-mouthed glass and passed the goblet under his nose, sniffing appreciatively. "Not at all, cher ami. From the first I did suspect there was something not altogether right about that house.

"To begin, you will recall that on the night Monsieur Van Riper took us from the station he told us his progenitor had imported the house, stone by single stone, to this country from Cyprus?''

"Yes,'' I nodded.

"Very good. The stones of which it is erected were probably quarried from the ruins of some heathen temple, and like sponges soaked in water, they were full to overflowing with evil influences. This evil undoubtedly affected the old warrior knights who dwelt in that house, probably from 1191, when Richard of England sold Cyprus to their order, to 1308, when the French king and the Roman pope suppressed and destroyed the order—and shared its riches between them.

"That the souls of those old monks who had forsaken their vows to the God of Love to serve the Goddess of Lust with unclean rites and ceremonies could not find rest in peaceful graves there is little doubt. But that they were able to materialize and carry on the obscenities they had practiced in life, there is also much doubt. Some ghosts there are who can make themselves visible at will; others can materialize at certain times and in certain places only; others can show themselves only with the aid of a medium.

"When the rich Monsieur Profiteer took up the old house and brought it to America, he doubtless imported all its evil influences intact; but they were latent.

"Then, only one little week ago, that which was needful came to the house. It was nothing less than Mademoiselle O'Shane's so beautiful self. She, my friend, is what the spiritualists call a sensitive, a psychic. She is attuned to the fine vibrations which affect the ordinary person not at all. She was the innocent medium through which the wicked knights were able to effect a reincarnation.

"The air may be filled with the ethereal waves from a thousand broadcasting stations, but if you have not a radio machine to entrap and consolidate those waves into sound, you are helpless to hear so much as a single squeal of static. Is it not so? Very good. Mademoiselle Dunroe was the radio set—the condenser and the amplifying agent needed to release the invisible wickedness which came from Cytherea's wicked altar—the discarnate intelligences which were once bad men. Do you not recall how she was greeted in the chapel of the Black Lodge: 'Hail, Priestess and Queen—She Who Gives Her Servants Life and Being?' Those wicked things which once were men admitted their debt to her in that salutation, my friend."

"Remember how Mademoiselle Dunroe told you of her inability to draw what she wished? The evil influences were already beginning to steal her brain and make her pliable to their base desires. They were beginning to lay plans to feed upon her vitality to clothe themselves in the semblance of humanity, and as they possessed her, she saw with her inward eye the scenes so many times heretofore enacted in that chapel."

"From the first I liked not the house, and when the poor Mademoiselle Dunroe told us of her troubles with her drawings, I liked it still less. How long it would have taken those old secret worshippers of evil to make themselves visible by the use of Mademoiselle Dunroe's vitality, I do not know. Perhaps they might never have succeeded. Perhaps she would have gone away and nothing more would have been heard of them, but that flap-eared she-ass of a Mademoiselle Prettybridge played the precise game the long-dead villains desired. When she held her so absurd seance in the dining-room that night, she furnished them just the atmosphere they needed to place their silent command in Mademoiselle O'Shane's mind. Her attention was fixed on ghostly things; 'Ah-ha,' says the master of the Black Lodge, 'now we shall steal her mind. Now we shall make her go into a trance like a medium, and she shall materialize us, and la, la, what deviltry we shall do!' And so they did.

While they sent one of their number to thump upon the table and hold us spellbound listening to his nonsense rimes, the rest of them became material and rode forth upon their phantom steeds to steal them a little child. Oh, my friend, I dare not think what would have been had they carried through that dreadful blood-sacrifice. Warm blood acts upon the wicked spirits as tonic acts on humans. They might have become so strong, no power on earth could have stayed them! As it was, the ancient evil could be killed, but it died very, very hard.''

"Was Dunroe under their influence when we saw her at the piano that night?" I asked.

"Undoubtedly. Already they had made her draw things she did not consciously understand; then, when they had roused her from her bed and guided her to the instrument, she played first a composition of beauty, for she is a good girl at heart, but they wished her to play something evil. No doubt the wicked, lecherous tune she played under their guidance that night helped mightily to make good, Godfearing Dunroe O'Shane forget herself and serve as heathen priestess before the heathen altar of a band of forsworn renegade priests.''

"H'm," I murmured dubiously. "Granting your premises, I can see the logic of your conclusions, but how was it you put those terrible ghosts to flight so easily?"

"I waited for that question," he answered. "Have you not yet learned Jules de Grandin is a very clever fellow?''

"Attend me, for what I say is worth hearing. When those evil men went forth in search of prey and killed the poor policeman, I said to me, 'Jules de Grandin, you have here a tough nut, indeed!' ''

" 'I know it,' I reply."

" 'Very well, then,' I ask me," 'who are these goblin child-stealers?'

" 'Ghosts—or the evil representations of wicked men who died long years ago in mortal sin,' I return.''

" 'Now,' I say, 'you are sure these men are materialized by Mademoiselle O'Shane—her strange playing, her unwitting drawings. What, then, is such a materialization composed of?' ''

" 'Of what some call ectoplasm, others psychoplasm,' I reply.''

" 'But certainly'—I will not give myself peace till I have talked this matter over completely—'but what is that psychoplasm, or ectoplasm? Tell me that?' ''

"And then, as I think, and think some more, I come to the conclusion it is but a very fine form of vibration given off by the medium, just as the ether-waves are given off by the broadcasting station. When it combines with the thin-unpowerful vibration set up by the evil entity to be materialized, it makes the outward seeming of a man—what we call a ghost.

"I decided to try a desperate experiment. A sprig of the Holy Thorn of Glastonbury may be efficacious as a charm, but charms are of no avail against an evil which is very old and very powerful. Nevertheless, I will try the Holy Thorn-bush. If it fail, I must have a second line of defense. What shall it be?"

"Why not radium salt? Radium does wonderful things. In its presence non-conductors of electricity become conductors; Leyden jars cannot retain their charges of electricity in its presence. For why? Because of its tremendous vibration. If I uncover a bit of radium bromide from its lead box in that small, enclosed chapel, the terrific bombardment of the Alpha, Tau and Gamma rays it gives off as its atoms disintegrate will shiver those thin-vibration ghosts to nothingness even as the Boche shells crushed the forts of Liege!"

"I think I have an idea—but I am not sure it will work. At any rate, it is worth trying. So, while Mademoiselle O'Shane lies unconscious under the influence of evil, I rush here with you, borrow a tiny little tube of radium bromide from the City Hospital, and make ready to fight the evil ones. Then, when we follow Mademoiselle Dunroe into that accursed chapel under the earth, I am ready to make the experiment."

"At the first door stands the boy, who was not so steeped in evil as his elders, and he succumbed to the Holy Thorn sprig. But once inside the chapel, I see we need something which will batter those evil spirits to shreds, so I unseal my tube of radium, and—pouf! I shake them to nothing in no time!"

"But won't they ever haunt the Cloisters again?" I persisted.

"Ah bah, have I not said I have destroyed them—utterly?" he demanded. "Let us speak of them no more."

And with a single prodigious gulp he emptied his goblet of brandy.

Two stories were published in WEIRD TALES by J. Wesley Rosenquest. As his name was not a familiar one in the pulps, it can be surmised that he was one of the many readers who occasionally submitted stories to "the unique magazine." Ambrose Bierce would have liked this short shocker.

RETURN TO DEATH

J. Wesley Rosenquest

Great sadness reigned in the little Transylvanian village of Rotfernberg; Herr Feldenpflanz was dead. Here and there, as one walked in the cob-blestoned streets, one saw a sudden dampness in the eyes of passers-by as his name was mentioned. Everyone was talking about him, praising his virtues, lamenting his early death; and in the eyes of many a fräulein was more than a trace of tears. He was indeed well beloved by all the village.

"Poor Herr Feldenpflanz," said the tailor sadly. "a fine man, as honest as the day is long. And a learned man, too. He went to the University of Berlin for four years, and knew more than any other man in Rotfernberg. Yes indeed, a very fine man."

The tailor blew his nose with vigor, and his listeners did likewise.

"And poor Fräulein Feldenpflanz! She loved her brother very dearly. She has no one else in the world. What will she do now?"

The tailor and his listeners all shook their heads sadly.

"Even now she sits beside him. For two days she has watched him, lying like life, so calm, and prays for his soul. We all know how he drifted away from God. Those wizard's things that he did in his big, white room! Tubes full of strange vapors and lights there were, and light-ning in glass balls. He always said that it was not magic—as if we had not eyes!"

"Yes," said the grocer sadly but with vigor, "as if we had not eyes!"

The village priest sat there also, a little outside the group, with sor-row written on his face; and every time one of the townsmen spoke of poor Herr Feldenpflanz's obvious traffic with Lucifer, an expression of deep pain passed over his mild and benign countenance. He was a short, stout, dark-haired man, and wore the vestments of his calling. He sat very calm and still. At last he could no longer listen without speaking his mind.

"Please, please," he said softly, "say no more of our good friend. He is now, I hope, among the blessed saints, and we must speak only well of the dead. Remember, he was a good man; perhaps he strayed without knowing that he was ensnared by the Enemy's wiles. If that be so, there is salvation for him. Let us not speak of Herr Feldenpflanz; let us not use our human judgment; let us rather pray with the Fräulein Feldenpflanz, who even now prays beside her brother's coffin."

So saying, he got up from his chair and motioned to the men gathered there in the tailor's store to follow him. They did so: the grocer, the tailor, the blacksmith, the butcher and the mayor. They climbed the steep mountain path with energy and puffing, and said nothing. The evening dew lay heavy on the long, wild grass; and from overhead fell cool drops from the leaves of the thick, ancient oaks growing on the mountainside. That cool, calm, mountain hush had descended with the twilight. It was as though a great, blue, star-sprinkled bowl had been inverted and placed upon the earth, with the summit of the mountain touching its spangled center.

Suddenly the priest spoke to his companions.

"See, my friends, there lies the Feldenpflanz dwelling. When we enter let us conduct ourselves with fitting dignity and propriety. We must not speak to the bereaved fräulein when we enter, but gather around the coffin and pray with her. We must not disturb her."

So it was. The big house, white-painted and gabled and surrounded by gardens, lay just before them. Marring the pure, solid color of the walls and the big front door hung a significant black ribbon. The calm hush was very pronounced here. In a window near the front door there twinkled a single electric light, the only one in the town of Rotfernberg. The unschooled villagers had always been amazed by the electric fixtures and the apparatus in Feldenpflanz's home and laboratory.

All silent, the group of men reached the end of the path and tried the door. It was open, and quietly they entered, Father Josef in the lead. They passed through a long, dark hall, at the end of which was a door leading into the parlor. Light gleamed through the crack along the floor. As they approached they heard the muffled sound of low praying, mingled with sobs.

Father Josef opened the door carefully and tiptoed in, followed by the five other villagers. They crossed themselves in unison.

₅By a simple, black coffin of wood knelt Fräulein Feldenpflanz. Under her knees was a cushion to make possible long vigils. Her face was hidden by her long, black hair, and her head hung low over the bier. Her pale lips moved constantly. At the head of the coffin, in spite of the electric light, burned a candle; the whole coffin itself was covered with mountain blooms. The heavy, cloying odor peculiar to death did not hang in the air, however. The kneeling woman cast one vacant, tearful glance at the entering men and resumed her former attitude.

The six men came close to the coffin and gazed down upon its occupant. There lay Herr Feldenpflanz, calm and handsome and indeed very life-like, dressed in a suit made by the tailor himself. They all knelt around the bier and prayed. . . .

As he lay there, Feldenpflanz, terrified by his predicament, could think of only one thing—escape. Ane one word echoed and re-echoed through his brain—catalepsy, catalepsy! . . .

For hours he had been forced to listen to his sister's prayers and tears; long hour after hour he heard his death mourned, and was unable to move. He felt his own heart-beat, very slow and very gentle so that no one would be able to detect it; but it sent the blood through his numbed brain, sustaining consciousness, so that, aware of all that went on, he could know the pangs of mortal fear and the bittersweet of faint hope. "Help! Help!" he tried to shout, but his mind alone formed the words; his lips defied his will.

An educated man, he knew the danger of his state. A chance existed that he might regain control of his limbs before he was buried—buried alive. Consciousness was a good sign, he knew. If now he could force his body to obey his will, the final stage of recovery from this dreadful malady, he would be saved; he would return to the world he loved, to life and living, to his sister Maria.

And then a terrifying thought flashed through his head. He realized that inevitably, if not soon, the air in his coffin would be exhausted! The oxygen of the air was slowly being used up; for although he did not move his chest, did not breathe, the air was entering and leaving his lungs by diffusion. If he could only move, a tap on the side of the box would attract attention and effect his release. Was he doomed to impotence and burial alive? The poor superstitious folk of Rotfernberg, including his sister, would probably flee in terror. It would be hopeless, then, even if he did recover the use of his limbs. They would leave him to struggle futilely in his flower-bedecked prison! Oh, why were these people not educated? Why must they confine themselves to a home and a mountainside?

Gradually he fell into a dreamy, reflective state, in which the first sharp agony of terror had dissolved away from sheer exhaustion; and only two hopes remained in his mind, like brilliant butterflies that rested for a brief moment on a withered flower. First, he must move; and second, his sister must not be afraid; she must set him free from his narrow prison. And these two hopes, bitter for their improbability and sweet for their possibility, were all for which he existed. . . .

To his ears still came the muffled voice of Maria, hoarse and weary from long use; through his eyelids the vigil-light shone. Suddenly he heard the sound of feet in the room where he was lying. He listened carefully; they were men, he calculated, about a half-dozen. Here was new hope! If he moved or made a sound, one of the men might have sense and courage enough to free him. Then his ears caught the sound of voices praying in unison. So now they too were praying for him!

Several minutes grew into an hour, and then the voices became still, including his sister's. A pang of apprehension ran through him like a red-hot sword. Were they going to leave him? But no. He heard the sound of scraping chairs and the rustle of clothing. They were sitting down. As he listened attentively, he heard a voice that was familiar, low-pitched though it was from respect for the dead, and muffled by the wooden walls that enclosed him. It was Father Josef.

"Please, Fräulein Feldenpflanz," he insisted gently, "you must go to bed now. You are very weary, and tomorrow you must rise early for your brother's funeral. Please sleep now."

There was no answer, but Feldenpflanz heard the sound of footsteps on the stairs. Maria was going upstairs, evidently.

"Let us hope," said Father Josef, "that our good friend has no need of our prayers. By now he is in Heaven or Hell. Be it not the latter."

The six men sat there quietly, nodding their heads.

"Or Purgatory," added the tailor, looking toward the priest for agreement.

The unmoving man in the coffin almost felt amused.

"After the burial the fräulein will no doubt destroy the unholy things in her brother's big, white room in the cellar," spoke up the blacksmith, who was a big man and who very seldom spoke. "I think," he continued, "that cellars should rightly hold only wines."

So they would like to see his laboratory destroyed! And after he was buried . . . He made a desperate, mighty attempt to move, but could not. Was it imagination or was the air really growing bad? His head began to swim, and he thought he felt his heart beat a little faster.

"The whole village of Rotfernberg will come to see the Feldenpflanz funeral," said the mayor, a tall, thin man, "and I will lead the procession. He was one of my best friends, and hence it is only fitting that I do so. Ah, well I remember his cheerful 'Good morning' and his fine wines. He was a generous man, too, always giving alms, and he paid the highest taxes in the town. No one was more honest, either. A very fine man."

The mayor blew his nose gently, as he was in the presence of the dead. All nodded their heads in agreement except Father Josef, who was absorbed in a prayerbook. His pale hands stood out against his black cassock, and his lips moved slightly; several minutes passed before he looked up.

"Dear God, dear God," prayed Feldenpflanz over and over as he felt the true death approaching. But what was this? He felt a tremor pass over his body. His heart beat faster, and a warm flush passed over his numbed limbs! Slowly, he felt his will creep down the sleeping nerves into his extremities. Very soon now, he hoped, freedom would be his.

"Let us go now," said the priest, and a pang of terror passed through the man in the coffin. He heard the scraping of chairs and the shuffling of feet. Now was the moment! Now he must move! The beating of his heart was tumultuous; his finger-tips were tingling; his face felt hot and his head full of blood. He heard the footsteps cease; they had evidently paused over him. He heard the rustle of clothing as they rubbed against the coffin. Then the butcher spoke, in a strained tone.

"How very life-like indeed! His face flushes with blood!"

Feldenpflanz made a supreme effort of will. The darkness seemed to shake—and his eyes were open! Above him he saw six faces in a frozen tableau.

Father Josef wore a look of utmost horror and shock.

The tailor's face, long and pale and drawn, wore an expression of fear and shocked suspicion.

The butcher opened eyes and mouth wide.

The grocer crossed himself again and again, his lips moving in frantic prayer.

The blacksmith, more afraid of the supernatural than the rest, closed his eyes, gasped, and staggered back.

The mayor stared for a moment with bulging eyes, then bawled out a single word:

"Vampire!"

Then there came the sound of running and shouting, and Feldenpflanz saw the faces disappear from above his prostrate form, except that of Father Josef, who was reading a Latin invocation from his prayerbook.

The cataleptic victim, now desperate, heard the noise of many feet running toward him, and the faces of the blacksmith and the butcher burst into view above him. There was a sound of fumbling at the side of the coffin, and then—the lid was raised. He was saved!

But what was this? The butcher had placed a knife against his left side, and the blacksmith raised a hammer high. There came to his ears the monotone of Father Josef's Latin prayer.

Feldenpflanz made inarticulate sounds.

"No, n' huh, huh, help, no!"

The hammer rose and fell. One! Two! Three!

Herr Feldenpflanz ceased to think of escape.

Robert Nelson was a young Illinois fan of WEIRD TALES who had several unusual poems published in the magazine before his untimely death at the age of seventeen. Farnsworth Wright thought very highly of his work, all of which has remained unreprinted until now.

UNDER THE TOMB

Robert Nelson

Dread beings grope and sport in gory lakes,
A foul mist creeps and feeds on swollen slugs;
From beds of perfumed plants squirm fetid snakes,
And like a flower grown from sable drugs,
A moon of steel drips blood upon a sky
Darkened by what mad phantoms prophesy.

But this hath ceased and passed, and now in that
Mephitic, crumbling woodland 'neath the tomb
The dead sup with the dead o'er flowing vat,
And searing candles cleanse the rotting gloom;
And they who stood in sorrow's joy and pain,
Tread now through hell's ecstatical refrain.

Far still beneath, where bloated babes are kept
In glacial rooms, and skulls are lit as lamps
To guide through life beyond, and where are swept
Green veils of oozing slime and deadly damps,
There is an everlasting resonance
Pealed by the tomb in glad deliverance.

FAR BELOW AND OTHER HORRORS

First Edition
1974

Far Below and Other Horrors, edited by Robert
E. Weinberg, was published by FAX Collector's
Editions, West Linn, Oregon. Approximately one
thousand copies of this first edition were printed
by CSA Press, Lakemont, Georgia from 10-point
Baskerville on Mohawk Creme-White Vellum and
bound in Holliston Black Roxite. Jacket art was by
Lee Brown Coye. Title page art was by Vincent
Napoli.